Judith,

May God bless
Family! I have +
getting to know + Sked with
you & your staff!
I hope you enjoy my books!

Tony Maney 2/22/2019

MW00529799

The Cop:
The Minister

The Twisted Road to Justice

Tony Korey

LifeRich
PUBLISHING

LifeRich Publishing is a registered trademark of The Reader's Digest Association, Inc.

LifeRich Publishing books may be ordered through booksellers or by contacting:

LifeRich Publishing
1663 Liberty Drive
Bloomington, IN 47403
www.liferichpublishing.com
1 (888) 238-8637

ISBN: 978-1-4897-1950-8 (sc)
ISBN: 978-1-4897-1951-5 (hc)
ISBN: 978-1-4897-1952-2 (e)

Library of Congress Control Number: 2018912250

Print information available on the last page.

LifeRich Publishing rev. date: 10/23/2018

ONE

It was Monday, March 11, 1974. Jack Caldwell had been promoted to detective two years ago, to the day. It still made him swell up with pride each time he looked at his bright gold-plated badge, which had the word Detective written in raised blue lettering, circling the top of the badge. It was a little smaller than the patrol badge, but it wasn't the size that mattered. The most important and impressive part was the fact that it had the word Detective and it was gold!

He suddenly got an eerie feeling. It felt like he was being watched. It was an instinct that had served Jack well for the past five years with the Atlanta Police Department. When he turned his head to the left, he could just catch the outline of a figure standing in the carport of his neighbor's house. Suddenly the carport light came on. Jack breathed a sigh of relief. It was just his neighbor, Ed Fincher.

Ed was a man who looked a lot older than his years. He had just turned fifty-one, but he appeared sixty-two, sixty-three, maybe more. Yet there was something stranger than this. As long as Jack had known him, which was admittedly only eighteen months, Ed Fincher had never seemed to change in his physical appearance. He still had those same deep lines in his cheeks. His skin was rough and leather-like, and his face was pock-marked. He had age spots on both arms and his neck was crepy and wrinkled.

Jack sat in his running car and studied his neighbor. *I think that's the same shirt he was wearing when I first met him,* Jack thought. *And the same haircut and the same slant to his shoulders. He never looks different. He must have been born an old man and simply stayed that way.*

Jack slowly backed out into the cul-de-sac. He noticed his neighbor's 1972 white Ford Fairlane also backing up. Jack quickly pulled out of the way. Ed would never look back. He was the epitome of the stubborn old man. He acted like he owned that cul-de-sac and everyone else in the neighborhood had better stay out of his way.

Jack politely waved when Fincher backed up close to him, missing his front passenger fender by mere inches. Fincher never acknowledged him as he slowly drove away.

He must really hate me, Jack thought. *I've been doing this for over a year and a half; and he's never acknowledged me.* It had become like a ritual to Jack. It had also become a challenge. For the past eighteen months, ever since he and his wife, Tammy, had moved into this newly developed neighborhood, Ed Fincher had said no more than ten words to them. The only time he spoke was to complain, usually about their cat, Ward, who would leave his mark on Ed's lawn. Jack would tell him that they would see what they could do with Ward and then disregard the complaint.

When Jack and his wife first moved into their new home on Park Lane, they were ecstatic. It was the first home they had ever owned. It was a small ranch-style house with a brick veneer front and a carport. Jack wanted to make friends with his neighbors, but it seemed as if Edwin Fincher wanted to have nothing to do with him or his wife.

At first Jack understood Ed Fincher's apprehension. He met Jack and his family under unique circumstances. Jack was assigned to the narcotics squad of the Atlanta Police Department. He was working an undercover assignment and had to appear to be a drug user and dealer. His hair was down to his shoulders, and he had a scraggly, unkempt beard and mustache. To make things worse, Jack smelled as bad as he looked. Jack was glad that assignment was over.

The rain seemed relentless as he pulled onto the expressway. He looked at the stream of headlights coming in the opposite direction. They seemed endless and appeared to be interlaced and sparkling in the steady rain. It was now 6:30 in the morning. It was the very beginning of spring.

"This sure is a nice way to begin the day," Jack said sarcastically. It didn't bother him that he was the only one in the car.

"I actually enjoy talking to myself!" he said with conviction.

He then turned toward the radio and fumbled with the buttons for a few minutes. He found his country station and settled in for the tedious stop-and-go drive into the city. His dull routine was suddenly shattered by the blaring horn behind him.

"What in the world is he doing?" The headlights of the car behind him seemed to disappear into his trunk.

Jack threw up his hands in disbelief.

"What do you expect me to do? It's rush hour." The subject behind him, however, continued to tailgate him.

Jack saw an opening when he passed an eighteen-wheel semi. He quickly darted to his right, barely missing the semi's left front bumper. As the tailgater pulled next to Jack, he noticed that there were two people in the vehicle. The passenger looked over at Jack. Jack's eyes locked in on the passenger window, which was being opened. It moved evenly and methodically. It did not have a jerking motion, and Jack also noticed that the passenger's arm and shoulder weren't moving.

Power window, Jack thought. *They just came out last year in the Chevy Camaro.* He then noticed the Z28 emblem on the right quarter panel. He also noticed the .45-caliber semiauto in the passenger's right hand as he raised it and began to point it toward Jack's closed window.

"He's got a gun!"

Jack slammed on his brakes. The passenger fired. The bullet grazed across the front hood of Jack's Galaxy. He immediately cut to the left. The result was pure pandemonium. When he moved to the left, he found himself directly behind the black 1974 Chevrolet Camaro Z28 that carried the gunman.

The eighteen-wheeler, directly behind him, also cut sharply to its left, almost at the same time as Jack. It then jackknifed, shutting down that portion of the expressway.

Caldwell's service revolver, a .38-caliber Smith & Wesson, was laying in the passenger seat. Next to it was a Browning 9 mm, his backup weapon. He started to grab the Browning but hesitated.

He had better call this in. "Unit 181 to radio."

"Go ahead, 181."

"I'm in pursuit of a black Chevy Camaro, southbound on I-75 from Barrett Parkway! Please let Cobb county know and tell them that I need help right away."

"Radio received; I'm advising Cobb right now. Do you need me to start any of our units in your direction?"

The morning watch captain interrupted.

"Go ahead."

"What's the problem here? Why do you need our units to go to Cobb County?"

"Two guys in the car are shooting at me. Is that reason enough?" Jack snapped.

"Don't get smart with me, Detective!" the captain snapped back. "Remember, I'm a captain."

Then the day watch captain interrupted.

"Go ahead, 202," radio answered.

"All day watch units are in service; go ahead and send any available day watch units to assist Detective Caldwell."

"Thank you, Captain Schackelford," Caldwell replied. It was the first time that someone had called him Detective all day. It felt pretty good.

The radio operator immediately responded. "All available day watch units start for Interstate 75 southbound between Barrett Parkway and the Chattahoochee Bridge to assist Unit 181. Shots are being fired by two white males. Both subjects are armed with .45-caliber black semiautomatic handguns. They are also wanted for aggravated assault against a law enforcement officer.

Detective Caldwell, Cobb County wants to know if the overturned semitruck and trailer are part of your incident?"

"Yes, it is," Caldwell answered.

At that time four day watch units responded to assist Detective Caldwell. Three morning-watch units offered to stay over if the day watch captain needed their assistance. John Schackelford, the day watch captain, thanked them but declined their offer.

Hiram Masters, the morning watch captain, immediately responded with, "I hope the three of you are ready to turn in your completed reports, since you're so anxious to help Cobb County. After all, we're the ones paying you, not Cobb!" It was obvious that his voice was stressed, and he was angry.

"This is James Banner," said Caldwell's partner. "I came on at the 120-loop entrance to the expressway, and I'm behind the black Camaro."

"All units hold nonemergency traffic!" radio snapped. "Go ahead, Detective Banner. What's your location?"

"I'm south on 75, approaching Northside Parkway and Paces Ferry Drive. This guy is driving like a madman; and he's wrecking cars left and right. The passenger is now shooting at me. Permission to use deadly force."

"Use any necessary force to stop them," Captain Schackelford answered.

"Hey James, I'm right behind you," said Caldwell. "Move over to the left. The driver has a gun, and he's getting ready to shoot at you through the rear windshield."

As if on cue, the rear windshield of the Camaro exploded as Banner was switching lanes. The .45-caliber round slammed through it and was headed directly toward Banner's front windshield. Banner instinctively leaned to his left, causing him to turn the steering wheel slightly to the left. It was enough to cause his right tire to rub against the Camaro's left bumper and the edge of his left rear tire. It was basically an unintentional pit maneuver. The Camaro immediately began to spin uncontrollably to the left. The chaos from the gunshots and reckless conduct of the two gunmen resulted in nearly ten miles of Interstate 75 resembling the carnage of a war zone. The vehicles in front of the Camaro sped away to escape the madhouse occurring behind them.

The passenger of the Camaro was thrown against the driver. The gun discharged, and the .45-caliber round struck the driver on the upper side of his left thigh, just below his pelvic bone.

"I can't believe it," screamed the driver. "You just shot me in the leg!" He then turned the steering wheel loose and automatically grabbed his wounded left thigh. The car continued to spin. The driver was so angry and in so much pain he pointed his gun at his partner, who had just shot him. The driver fired twice.

The first shot struck his partner in the left shoulder; and the second grazed the left side of his neck.

"What are you doing!" Screamed his partner. "You're trying to kill me!!!"

"You're absolutely right!" snapped the driver; ignoring the second complete spin of the Camaro, which now slammed against the median wall. The impact caused the driver to be thrown into the passenger. The barrel of the driver's gun, which was in his right hand, was now touching his partner's forehead.

"You deserve this," the driver said, very calmly, as he pulled the trigger; killing his partner instantly.

As the driver leaned back to admire his handiwork; he felt the cold nickel-plated barrel of Caldwell's. Semi-automatic hand-gun touching his right temple.

"I hope you have a steady hand," Caldwell said. "If that gun so much as twitches, your soul will be on its way to be judged."

Banner reached in and snatched the gun from the driver's hand.

"You need to call me an ambulance," the driver said.

"Why?" Caldwell asked.

"I've been shot," he said as he lifted his left hand which covered the hole in his upper thigh.

"What in the world.," Banner said. "That looks serious. That looks like a lot of paperwork." His tone was both sarcastic and cold. "I sure am glad that I didn't do it," Banner said, as he smiled, and looked directly at his partner.

"It wasn't me," Caldwell said. "I think they shot each other."

"You're right," Banner answered. He opened the passenger door, shoved the dead occupant against the driver and ripped the driver's pant leg open with a small pocket knife; to better see the wound. He then pushed on the wound with the same knife.

"Are you blind!" the driver screamed. "That's where I'm shot! I need an ambulance! Keep your filthy hands off me!"

"The trouble with you," Caldwell said to Banner, as he lifted Banner's hand and knife away from the driver's wound, "is the fact that you're not sensitive to this man's needs."

It was as if they could read each other's minds. Banner moved his left hand to the driver's mouth and clamped it shut. He then shoved the pocket knife through the seat belt and next to the driver's right pelvic bone. The driver was so terrified that he nearly went into shock. His scream was so loud that the four officers trying to clear the expressway of the multiple wrecks, stopped and started running towards them. Caldwell raised his hand and indicated for them to stop.

"We're okay, guys," Caldwell yelled. "The driver's trapped and we're trying to cut him loose from the seat belt." The officers waved and went back to work.

Caldwell then pulled out his $2.00 Bic Ball Point pen from his shirt pocket and lit the tip with his cigarette lighter.

"I believe in sterilization," said Caldwell, with a slight laugh. "Don't worry," said Caldwell, as he pulled a notebook from the same shirt pocket. "I need to get some information from you."

"I ain't saying nothing without a lawyer," the driver said, emphatically.

"That's fine," Banner responded. "In the meantime, I want you to look behind you. What you see is nothing but chaos. The entire expressway is completely shut down. The only emergency vehicle that can probably get through is a Life-Flight helicopter. The only way that will happen, however, is if we request it. Do you understand what I am saying?"

The driver nodded, indicating that he understood.

"We are now going to ask you some questions," said Caldwell. "The quicker you truthfully answer these questions; the quicker we will be able to request a Life-Flight."

"Whatda you want to know?" The driver gasped.

It took nearly thirty minutes for the ambulances to finally arrive at the scene. It only took fourteen minutes for life-Flight to arrive. They life-flighted the driver to Grady Memorial Hospital. The passenger was sent to the morgue. Both Caldwell and Banner spent the rest of the day on paperwork; but they smiled at each other, knowing they had the information they needed.

"Would you have actually shoved that pen into his wound?" Banner asked Caldwell.

"Of course not." answered Caldwell. "That would have put us at his level."

"I'm glad to hear that," smiled Banner.

Two

"Do you honestly expect me to believe that you weren't trying to intimidate the driver of the vehicle by holding your ballpoint pen over his wound? asked Lt. Hines of the Internal Affairs Division. "Then your partner almost stuck a dirty pocket knife into the gentleman's hip, while attempting to cut off the seat belt/"

"I really don't care what you believe," answered Caldwell. "That's exactly what happened. The only difference is the fact that my partner, Detective Banner, tried to cut the seat belt off before I pulled out my pen to take notes. I was also trying to find a cloth or something to use as a tourniquet. Then I could use the pen to twist the cloth tightly to stop the bleeding. In the meantime, James was trying to cut off the seat belt, which was jammed,"

"If you don't start telling us the truth," said Sgt. Rick Gaines, Hines' partner; "then we can't protect you."

"So, you're trying to protect me?" laughed Caldwell.

Suddenly the interview was interrupted by a sharp knock at the door.

"Whoever you are," shouted Hines. "You have to wait until we're finished. We're in the middle of an interview."

"You better be a Lieutenant, or above," yelled Gaines, as he opened the door, "or you're in a lot of trouble."

Gaines's jaw dropped, and Hines jumped to attention when Major Bobby Moore, the commander of the Special Operations Division;

which included the Intelligence and Internal Affairs Units, stepped into the room.

"Your investigation is over!" said Moore as he gathered IA's notes from the interview table and threw them into the hallway. "Now pick up your junk, and get out of here"

"Yes sir," said Hines, jumping towards the doorway, trying to beat Gaines out of the office. They both arrived at the same time. Hines punched Gaines in the stomach and shoved him backwards.

"I guess he's letting him know that he's the Lieutenant," said Moore, laughing, as they both stumbled out of the room. Moore then slammed the door shut behind them.

"Are you okay, Jack?" asked Moore as he extended his hand.

"I'm better, now," said Caldwell, shaking the Major's hand. "But to what do I owe the honor of your company?"

"Do you know who the guys were who tried to kill you and your partner?" asked Major Moore.

"Yes sir. I do," said Caldwell. "I know everything about them."

"Then tell me what you know, so far," Moore said. "Besides the fact that they were hit men for the Dixie Mafia."

Bobby Moore was one of the best intelligence commanders in the country. In fact, agencies from all over the United States would send officers to his specialized courses on counter intelligence. He was touted as being the Father of Counter-Intelligence.

Caldwell nodded. "You are exactly right, Major."

"What did you do that upset them so much?" asked Moore.

"I suppose it has something to do with that incident in Jacksonville," answered Caldwell.

"That's exactly what I thought," said Moore. "Was it Vernon Kimbrel who hired them?"

Caldwell nodded. "I had no doubt that it was."

Major Bobby Moore leaned over and touched Caldwell on the arm. "I hope you realize it, by now, that I'm on your side," he said. "I protected you for the past five years; and I don't intend to stop now." He continued. "I don't care how you got the information. I love the fact that you could get it. You are one absolutely smart detective."

Caldwell smiled. "Thank you, sir! That means a lot to me. Especially coming from you."

A unique bond formed between Major Bobby Moore and Detective Jack Caldwell on the day that he and Banner had become members of the Special Operations Unit, five years earlier. That bond remained and would remain in place for the remainder of all three of their lives. Bobby Moore's uncanny ability to analyze any situation catapulted him from the rank of Sergeant to Major in less than five years. He was now being groomed for the position of Superintendent of Patrol Operations.

"I wonder if they gave Kimbrel a money back guarantee?" laughed Moore.

"I'm sure that Kimbrel's going to want Knowles to finish the job or give him back what he spent," Caldwell said.

"Has he already paid them?" The Major asked.

"Five thousand now, and another five when it's done."

"Each?" asked Moore.

Caldwell simply nodded. "I guess he figured that killing a cop would take two hit-men."

"What about your partner?" Moore's voice sounded more serious.

Caldwell looked up at Moore and asked, "What do you mean?"

"Did they say that they were hired to only kill you, or was Banner part of the contract?"

Caldwell stood up and took a deep breath. His brow furrowed; he had a strained look upon his face.

"What's wrong?" Asked Moore

"I trust you, Major." Caldwell looked directly at him. "I'm going to tell you everything; but I don't think I need to tell you how I got Knowles to talk. Am I right in saying that?"

Bobby Moore stood up and put his hand on Caldwell's shoulder. "You're absolutely right in saying that." He said. "As I already told you; I'm on your side; and I don't care how you got the information. These worthless thugs tried to kill two cops! You and your partner!"

Jack Caldwell breathed a sigh of relief. "Thank you, Sir."

They then both sat down, and Caldwell told the Major, in detail, everything that Knowles had said about the plot to kill him; and the reasons why Vernon Kimbrel wanted it done. He told the whole story; from beginning to end; and Major Bobby Moore listened intently.

THREE

VERNON KIMBREL WAS 22 YEARS OLD WHEN HE JOINED THE DIXIE Mafia. He started off as a burglar. In just a few short years he became a career criminal. He advanced rapidly through the ranks. He was most notorious for "cracking safes. He openly bragged that there wasn't a safe made that he could not open.

Jack Caldwell was first introduced to Kimbrel during his senior year at Jacksonville University in Jacksonville, Florida. Jack's college roommate was Jimmy Counter. Counter had grown up with Kimbrel and had a strange admiration for Kimbrel's seeming fearlessness. What Counter mistook for "fearlessness," however, was the fact that Vernon Kimbrel was a sociopath. Kimbrel cared about no one or anything but himself, and he felt absolutely no remorse or guilt for any harm he would cause.

Jimmy Counter would constantly tell stories about Kimbrel, all of them having the same moral: he dared anyone to stop him from doing whatever he wanted. He once described to Jack a summer day when Jimmy was only fourteen and Kimbrel was almost seventeen. They were riding their bikes through downtown Jacksonville on their way to a movie theatre. Suddenly, a handicapped young man in a wheelchair cut in front of Kimbrel's path. Kimbrel stopped his bike and quietly got off.

Jimmy Counter looked on, with horror, as Vernon Kimbrel grabbed the young man's wheelchair, with him still in it, and shoved it into the busy downtown street. Then without saying a word; he jumped back on his bike and darted down the nearest alleyway, completely undetected. When Counter finally caught up with him, Kimbrel simply laughed. "That'll teach that kid to watch where he's going next time!"

"He was hit by a car!" Jimmy yelled to Kimbrel. "Several other cars wrecked trying to keep from hitting him, because he was in a wheelchair."

"Did you tell them that I did it?" Kimbrel's voice sounded both cracked and sinister. When he looked at Counter, his eyes had a cold deathly appearance. His look was so intense and terrifying that a cold chill went straight up Counter's spine.

"Of course, not!" Jimmy answered, with a miserable fake laugh that followed. "I've always got your back, Vernon. You know that."

Jimmy Counter was twenty-nine now and attending college to get a business degree. He was about to inherit his father's RV business; but his father insisted that he get a degree beforehand. Jimmy would be getting his degree in less than six months; then his money troubles would be over.

One afternoon, when Jack and Jimmy were watching a Jacksonville University basketball game, there was a loud knock at their apartment door. It was followed by a loud voice: "It's the cops, open up."

Jimmy calmly looked over at Jack. "Don't worry. I know who it is."

When Jimmy unlocked the door, Jack noticed that the person invited in was a tall lanky man wearing a black fake leather jacket. The jacket was costume-like, with its rhinestones around the edge and along its collar. The man also had slicked back dark hair, which appeared to be held in place by grease. Kimbrel appeared to be a lot older than his age of thirty-one. His efforts to make himself look younger had miserably failed. He wore wide horned-rim glasses, which added even more years to his appearance. His over-sized glasses kept slipping down his nose, causing him to continuously push them back into place. The result was a slight bruise above the bridge of his nose. His dark brown eyes seemed to be constantly moving, as if he were surveying the entire room; and added even more to his shifty appearance.

When he stepped in, Jimmy said, "Vernon, this is my roommate Jack Caldwell. Jack this is my dearest friend Vernon Kimbrel."

Jack got up from the recliner and stuck out his hand. "I'm glad to meet you," Caldwell said. Vernon slightly hesitated in returning the handshake. "Yeah," he coldly answered.

It was then that Jack noticed the over-sized medallion-shaped brass belt buckle pushed forward because of Kimbrel's slightly oversized stomach. There were two large initials, also in burnished brass. *VK.*

"Why don't you grab a seat and watch the game with us?" Jimmy asked Vernon.

"I can't. I only came by to give you this." Vernon then handed Jimmy a fat brown envelope. "It's the loan you requested."

A smile came across Jimmy's face.

"This is great," said Jimmy, taking the envelope. "I don't know how to thank you."

"Yes, you do," said Vernon. "Just pay it back with interest."

"Don't worry about that," said Counter. "You'll get it back with interest in plenty of time."

"I'm not worried," said Kimbrel, as he lifted the front of his fake leather jacket to reveal the butt of a .357 magnum handgun, just to the right of his 'VK' belt buckle. "I'm sure that you'll get it all back to me; either one way or another." He then laughed.

It was in that instant that Jack Caldwell knew that Vernon Kimbrel was a dangerous man. He also realized that he was capable of anything. He hated the thought that his roommate was now in debt to such a man.

"I suppose that's your initials," Jack said, pointing at the buckle.

"I like to think of it as my obligation!" Kimbrel said, with a sinister smile, which reflected his two gold front teeth. One tooth had a 'V' and the second had a 'K' engraved in the gold. "I like to think of myself as a Virgin Killer." His sinister smile was now joined by an equally sinister laugh.

When Kimbrel finally left, Caldwell asked his roommate directly, "What in the world do you think you're doing?"

"I know this seems crazy," answered Counter. "I might be inheriting my dad's business in just a couple of months; but I need money now to plan for my wedding." Jimmy looked down, ashamed. "I didn't know what else to do!" He appeared on the verge of tears.

Jack Caldwell's heart went out to Jimmy Counter. For a roommate who seemed to always have it together, it now appeared that Jimmy Counter was on the edge of destruction.

"Don't worry," said Jack Caldwell, putting his arm around his roommate. "We'll get through this. After all we are in this together."

Counter smiled. "Thanks. I needed to hear that."

"Everything's going to be fine," Caldwell said, oblivious to the terror ahead.

That next morning Jack made his usual trip from his apartment to the student center, where he would meet his other friend—also named Jimmy.

"I wonder if I read too many Marvel Comic Books growing up," Jack said to himself. Superman's friend was also named 'Jimmy.'

"Over here!" Jimmy Banner called out to Jack, as he stepped into the student center.

Jack smiled and waved towards his future partner.

"What's up?" Banner asked.

"Same O, same O." Jack's response was automatic; he slumped into the over-stuffed leather chair next to Banner's.

It was a ritual which they both truly enjoyed. They would arrive at the student center before 7:00 am, when very few of the other students were even up. They would then enjoy a freshly made cup of coffee, intended for the staff, but which included them, ever since their "heroic" actions, two years earlier.

Early one evening, those two years earlier, just after it turned dark, both Caldwell and Banner were walking towards their cars in the student center parking lot. The center was just getting ready to close when Jimmy realized that he had left his wallet on the counter next to the pool table.

"I need to go back and get it," said Banner.

"Hold up!" said Jack. "I'll go with you."

As they both walked back to the center, Jack noticed a black Volkswagen parked next to the entrance of the Student center. Two figures were seated in the front of the vehicle. Jack had an eerie feeling.

"Wait a minute," said Jack, touching Jimmy's arm.

"What's wrong?" asked Banner.

"I don't know," Caldwell replied.

Suddenly the lights to the student center went out; and shortly after that the front door opened. Jennifer Cumming, the center manager, stepped out and began to lock the door.

Jimmy Banner started to call out to her, when Jack grabbed his shoulder.

"Don't say a word," whispered Jack; he pulled him into the shadows next to the trees. "They're going to rob her," he softly said.

"Who?" asked Jimmy.

Jack reached down and picked up a rock next to the base of a tree. "The two guys in the VW," whispered Jack.

Banner pulled a switchblade from his pocket and popped it open.

Both men got out of the VW. Ski-masks hid their faces. At first, Jennifer didn't notice them, since she was busy putting her keys back in her purse. She dropped them next to a large money bag, which contained the day's receipts and money from the student center activities.

Jack circled behind the car and managed to come up behind the two, who were now brandishing hand-guns. Banner walked directly towards Jennifer, acting oblivious to the two would-be robbers.

"Hey, Jennifer!" yelled Jimmy. "I need back in …"

Both men turned towards Banner, not noticing Caldwell, directly behind them. Jennifer saw what was happening and screamed. One of the gunmen turned and pointed his gun at her. Jack, instinctively, hit him as hard as he could, against the left temple of his head, causing him to crumble to his feet with a sickening groan. The second gunman raised his gun towards Jack's head. Jimmy rushed the second robber, stabbing his right hand with his knife; causing him to drop his gun.

The first gunman remained two years later in a coma, set to be tried, when, if he ever recovers. The second one is serving a forty-year sentence for his conviction of the armed robbery.

"Well, how are my two heroes doing?" asked Jennifer Cummings, as she placed the tray down on the table. It contained two cups of coffee, two sweet rolls, and two plates of ham and eggs, with toast.

"Jen, you can't continue doing this," said Banner. "This is costing you way too much money. We can pay for our own breakfast."

"I know," she said; "but how much do you think my life is worth?"

Both Caldwell and Banner nodded.

"We understand," said Caldwell. "We love you, Jennifer Cummings; and we'll always love you, whether you serve us breakfast or not."

"So, you want me to stop?"

"I did not say that!" Caldwell emphasized. "This character next to me is the only one who mentioned that."

Jennifer flipped her beautiful blond hair away from her hazel eyes and burst out laughing. Although she was twenty-eight, Jennifer did not appear to be a day over eighteen. Her white shorts and red halter constantly drove both Jimmy and Jack to cold showers each morning.

"So, I guess you're still married," Jack said; already knowing the answer.

"Yes, Jack!" Jennifer answered. "Still very happily married, as I was yesterday, last week, and last year, when you first asked." She then gave him a smile and seductively blew him a kiss.

Jack then turned towards Jimmy, giving a half-hearted smile.

"What's wrong?" asked Banner. "I've seen that look before. It's your 'I've gotten myself into some mess and don't know how to get out,' look."

"It's nothing," Jack replied. "It's just something that we have to go through."

"What do you mean by 'we'?" asked Banner. "Never mind," he said. "I know you're talking about. Counter. That guy is nothing but trouble. He must be twenty-seven or twenty-eight years old," Banner guessed.

"Almost twenty-nine," Jack interrupted. "His birthday is the tenth of next month. If we have a party, do you want to come."

"That's not the point," Jimmy shouted.

The students in the center suddenly quieted.

"This is private," Jimmy yelled to everyone in the center. "It doesn't concern you, so go back to your business."

Some laughter was heard; and everyone went back to their activities.

"Just tell me the problem," Banner said, in a very frustrated tone.

Caldwell nodded. He then told him about Kimbrel and the money that Counter had borrowed. He also described Kimbrel and the gun which he had tucked in his waist. Caldwell also explained his fears of both Kimbrel and Counter's hopes of inheriting his father's business in order to pay back the loan.

"So, what happens if he doesn't pay it back?" asked Banner.

"That's why Kimbrel showed us the gun," Caldwell said. "He indicated that it was his insurance that Counter would pay his debt and interest back on time."

"And how much time is that?" asked Banner.

"I don't know. Neither Jimmy nor Kimbrel ever said."

"Well, at least you're not in this!" Banner said, with a sigh of relief.

Caldwell looked at the floor and slowly put his head in his hands.

"Come on, Jack!!!" Banner blurted out. "Please don't tell me that you are in this."

Caldwell simply nodded. "I told Jimmy Counter that we were in this together. I'm sorry, James. I'm not trying to put you in the middle of it, too. I just needed someone to talk to."

"I know, my friend," said James Banner. "I know. Don't worry about anything. We'll figure something out. Besides, it may not be as bad as we think. Counter might actually inherit the company; and pay Kimbrel back; and we would have done all this worrying for nothing."

Caldwell looked towards Banner and shook his head. He knew that even Banner didn't believe a word that he just said.

FOUR

Seven weeks later, Caldwell and Banner would get their answer. Jimmy Counter failed a required course and would not graduate at the end of the Spring Semester. Making matters worse; the economics course he failed was not offered in the Summer Semester. Even if he took and passed it in the Fall Semester, he would have to wait until then to receive his degree.

"I can't believe it!" screamed Counter, pounding the table with his fist.

"Please, honey; don't let yourself get all upset." Sheila, his bride of three weeks, softly said. "The good news is you don't have to go to school this summer; and you don't have to run your daddy's business; so, we can now take our delayed Honeymoon." She then giggled like a schoolchild, hugging him. Jimmy Counter pulled her closer to keep her from seeing his expression. He then looked at Caldwell and Banner and rolled his eyes. Sheila was completely clueless to the deal between him and Kimbrel.

Jack nodded to Counter, indicating that he understood. Jimmy Banner, meanwhile, stood up.

"Well, I have to get to the 'paper'," said Banner, who was a reporter for the Jacksonville Journal and Florida Times Union. "My shift starts in 45 minutes."

"I'll walk out with you," said Caldwell to his new roommate. Since Counter got married, Caldwell and Banner had decided to become roommates for the rest of the summer semester. Counter simply moved out and moved in with Sheila; and Banner moved in and took Counter's place. Since Banner spent most of his time at Caldwell and Counter's place, it seemed like nothing had changed.

"Well, I guess we'll have a better idea tonight," said Caldwell. "Jimmy is supposed to meet Kimbrel at 7:30 pm at the Waffle House on Arlington."

"I'm sure it will be alright," Banner said. "I don't think he'd kill him in that Waffle House. It's usually crowded with Jacksonville University students."

"You're right. He might die from eating "Bert's Chili, but I don't think that Kimbrel would chance hurting him there."

"Just to be safe," said Banner; "I might swing by there with a couple of my cop friends. After all, I do work the police beat; and I do have to do some follow-up work on a couple of stories I'm writing."

"Just don't let Kimbrel get suspicious."

"How is he going to get suspicious?" asked Banner. "I've never seen him and he's never seen me."

Caldwell smiled and nodded as Banner got into his 1965 green Mustang convertible and drove off. It was 2:45 pm when James Banner pulled into the back-parking lot, marked "Employees Only", of the Journal Times Union. He had 15 minutes before his shift started. That would give him enough time to grab his afternoon coffee from the employees' lounge on his way up to the fourth floor, the location of the City Desk. It was 2:58 pm when Banner stepped off the elevator onto his turf.

"Well, good afternoon, Mr. Banner," said Brince Thomas, the evening managing editor.

The City Desk was the very heart of the newspaper. The City Desk Managing Editor would decide whether to approve or disapprove all assignments. The managing editor would also determine who handled the assignment and wrote the story, as well as the story's placement—i.e., national, metro, or local. Brince Thomas might be the Evening Managing Editor of the City Desk today, but he was slated to become the Executive Managing Editor after Frank Collingsworth retired from the position in four weeks.

"Good afternoon, boss," said Banner. "Just going to check in."

Thomas only nodded.

Banner found his time card and clocked in at exactly 3:00 pm. He then went to his mail box and pulled out several junk mail letters and a note. Banner quickly opened the note. "See Me about the Police/Sheriff Merger!" Br T.

Banner walked back to the City Desk, holding the note.

"You wanted to see me about this, Mr. Thomas?" asked Banner.

Thomas took the note from Banner's hand and looked at it.

"Oh, yes!" said the City Editor. "I want you to see the Chief of Police and the Sheriff and get their opinions on the scheduled merger of their departments next week."

"No problem," said Banner.

"By the way, James," said Thomas," I picked you because I really liked that piece you did last month on the police officers' apprehension to that 'Miranda Warning.'" Thomas smiled.

It was the first time in the year of Banner's employment with the paper that he had seen Thomas do anything but scowl. In fact, it was the first time that Thomas had ever called him by his first name. Banner just stood there, speechless, with a stupid smile on his face.

Thomas looked at him. "Okay, son," he said. "You have to get this done by nine thirty tonight; so, you better get started."

James Banner, now flustered, turned and started towards the elevator. He immediately stopped. First he had to make appointments to speak to both the Chief of Police and the Sheriff. His face was bright red, with embarrassment, as he walked past the City Editor's Desk.

Thomas just smiled and shook his head. Banner's embarrassment eased, however, as he realized that meeting with the Chief of police and Sheriff could solve his other problem of being there when Counter met with Kimbrel.

"I'll be glad to meet you at the Waffle House," said Buck Lance, the Chief of the Jacksonville Police Department when Banner called him after arranging a separate, earlier appointment with the Sheriff. "I don't know if you knew it or not; but that's one of my favorite eating spots."

"Mine too," answered Banner.

"Great! See you there at 7:15."

The meeting with the Sheriff, Dale Parsons, went as expected. He praised the merger and expounded on how it would save the tax payers so much money and expand the tax base.

"Jacksonville-Duval County will, literally be the largest city in the nation," said Parsons. "The merger would not only increase our jurisdictional boundaries; it would also enhance our capabilities!" Parsons sounded like he was talking to a room full of voters, instead of one lone reporter seated across his desk.

"I can tell that you're very much in favor of the merger," Banner stated.

"You're right I am. It's the best thing that's happened to Jacksonville and Duval County since its founding."

"Can I quote you on that?" asked Banner.

"You sure can!" nodded the Sheriff. "Just make sure you spell my name right," he laughed. "It's Parsons: P A R S O N S." He meticulously sounded each letter.

"Should I say sheriff?" quipped Banner.

"Of course, ... Oh, I get it. I like you, Jimmy," laughed the Sheriff. "You have a sense of humor like mine."

Banner then stood up and shook the Sheriff's hand.

"The story will be in the morning edition and the day-time edition of the Times Union," Banner said. "In all probability, it will also run in the afternoon edition of the Journal."

"I'll look forward to reading it," said the Sheriff, shaking Jimmy's hand goodbye.

It was 7:05 by the time Jimmy Banner pulled into the Waffle House parking lot. A brand new black 1966 Ford Fairlane pulled into the lot at the same time. Chief Lance and another officer were in the vehicle. Although it wasn't marked, the looped antenna and the blue and red lights in the grill, as well as the blue "Bubble-Gum Machine" light, as it was called, on the dash, identified it as a police vehicle. Jimmy waited in his Mustang to give the Chief and his officer a chance to go in and get settled.

When Jimmy walked into the restaurant, he found the Chief and the officer were seated at the back of the restaurant with their backs to the wall of a booth. Several waitresses and the manager were around them. The waitresses were giggling, the manager was introducing "his friend" the Chief to them and some of the customers. Jimmy walked up to the booth and stuck out his hand.

"Chief Lance?" Jimmy politely asked.

The Chief and the officer started to stand; Jimmy motioned for them to stay seated.

"There's no need to do that, sirs. You both just got seated," said Jimmy. "I'm Jimmy Banner, with the Journal-Times Union."

"Happy to meet you, Jimmy," replied the Chief, grabbing his hand and shaking it. "This is Captain Johnny Hunt, my evening watch commander."

Banner nodded at the Captain and shook his hand. Banner sat across from the two, and they all ordered.

The Chief was totally against the merger.

"I'm not sure this merger is going to do any good for the citizens of Jacksonville," the Chief said; he then asked his Captain, "What do you think, Johnny?"

Hunt simply nodded. "I couldn't agree with you more."

"Why do you say that?" asked Jimmy, taking meticulous notes. Banner also kept glancing at the mirror at the back of the Waffle House above the two officers' booth. He was waiting to see when Kimbrel and Counter met.

The Chief and Capt. Hunt went on to explain how the merger would impact so many jobs because of the "so called duplication of duties." That was Lance.

"Besides," captain Hunt emphasized, "who is supposed to be in charge? The Chief or the Sheriff. We can't have two bosses, can we?"

The Chief nodded. "I don't think the citizens of the city of Jacksonville, Florida, are going to want the Duval County Sheriff to run their City Police Department, "he emphatically said.

As Banner glanced out of the window he saw Jimmy Counter's Chevy Impala pull into the parking lot. It was exactly 7:30 pm. A bright red, 1962 Cadillac convertible, with loud mufflers, driven by Vernon Kimbrel, pulled in behind him.

Both Chief Lance and Capt. Hunt noticed Banner looking out the window.

"Is there something going on out there?" asked the Chief.

"No," answered Banner. "The muffler on that car just distracted me."

"It did seem a little loud," the Chief replied. "Have one of your officers check it out," the Chief told Hunt.

"Will do," the Captain acknowledged.

Both the Captain and the Chief went through numerous talking points which emphasized the problems with the merger. At one time, as the interview developed, Kimbrel got a little loud. Although he and Counter were seated in a booth near the entrance of the restaurant, they were heard by both the Chief and the Captain.

"Do you want me to check it out?" the Captain asked the Chief.

"Let's not be in too much of a hurry," the Chief said. "They seem to be calming down, now that they noticed us."

Banner could see Kimbrel in the mirror raising his hands and mouthing the words "I'm sorry," to Captain Hunt.

"I see what you mean," said Hunt.

"Well I need to get my story written and turned in," said Banner, as he stood up and thanked the two officers. He told them when it would appear and promised to spell their names correctly. They all laughed, and Banner left to get back to the paper.

It was exactly 9:25 pm when Banner turned in the finished story to Brince Thomas.

"Do you always like to cut things this close?" Thomas said with a smile.

"I like to think of it as five minutes early," laughed Banner. "I hope it meets your approval, sir."

FIVE

THE NEXT MORNING JAMES BANNER WENT TO THE FRONT DOOR OF his apartment and got the morning edition of the Florida Times Union. To his surprise, it was the lead story on the front page.

"Wow," said Banner. "It made the front page!"

"What did?" asked Caldwell, as Banner stepped in and closed the front door.

"My story about the merger between the Sheriff and Police," answered Banner. "I thought it was a good story," he said, "but this … That's the first time I've ever had a 'Front Page' story; especially one with my own by-line."

The headline read:

> **"PUBLIC SAFETY MERGER CAUSES CONFLICT BETWEEN POLICE CHIEF AND SHERIFF: By James Banner, Staff writer.**

"That's neat," said Caldwell. "I'm living with a celebrity."

"What's the latest on Jimmy Counter?" Banner didn't want to make too big a deal of it, folding the paper and setting it aside.

"He called last night and said he was still alive. He also said that he was glad that you and those cops were there. You probably saved his life."

"Did Kimbrel threaten him?" asked Banner.

"Of course, he did," said Caldwell. "Said something about having to work for Kimbrel for the rest of his life."

"What? What did he mean by that?"

"I'm not sure," Caldwell answered. "He's supposed to come by here later today."

"Can you see if he could do it now?" asked Banner. "I have class in about two hours; and I have to be at work by three."

"Sure," said Caldwell; as he dialed Jimmy Counter's number.

Banner drummed his thumbs, picked back up the paper. The class this afternoon was Creative Writing; and he wanted to see and hear his fellow students' and professor's reaction to his front-page story. He, also, was anxious to hear what Brince Thomas had to say.

"He said that he'll be here in thirty minutes. He seemed very anxious to talk to us." Caldwell's voice sounded concerned. "He also said that he really needed our help."

"Did he say why?" asked Banner.

Caldwell shook his head. "I guess we'll find out when he gets here.

It was 8:30 am when Counter knocked at the door of Caldwell's and Banner's apartment door.

"Well, it's about time," chided Banner. "I have to meet my classmates at eleven; and I'll probably be signing autographs."

"What?" said Counter looking very confused. "I don't understand?"

"Don't listen to him," interrupted Caldwell. "His head has gotten so big, since he wrote that front page article, that he can hardly stand himself." Caldwell motioned for Jimmy Counter to have a seat in one of the over-stuffed leather chairs.

"I see you kept the chairs," Counter smiled.

Both Caldwell and Banner only nodded.

"So, what's up?" asked Banner. "I see you're still alive," he said half-laughing in a failed attempt to break the somber mood.

"Probably not for long," Jimmy Counter responded. He then went on to explain how Kimbrel got both cold and angry when he found out that he wouldn't get his money back for a while. At one point, he even yelled a threat of killing him, as he appeared to be reaching for his gun.

"He suddenly stopped, and looked past my shoulder," said Counter. "I wasn't sure what he was looking at, so I glanced in the mirror behind him and could see that it was two cops, who were sitting there with you." He nodded to Jimmy Banner. "I was never so glad to see anyone, in my life, as I was to see the three of you." Counter's eyes welled up as he once more nodded to Banner.

Banner smiled and returned the nod. "So, what happened after I left?" asked Banner.

"He got up about five minutes after you," said Counter. "Said that we really couldn't discuss business here, so he'd see me in the morning. I asked him where; but he didn't answer. He just got up and walked out. Leaving me with the bill."

"Did he come by this morning?" asked Caldwell.

"He sure did," Counter nodded. "He started beating on my door at 6:00 am. It's a good thing that Sheila had just left to go to work at the hospital."

"What did he say?" asked Banner; anxious to get to the bottom of the story.

Jimmy Counter looked down and shook his head in despair.

"He said that since I owed him so much money, and I couldn't pay it back, I had to work it off."

Counter went on to explain the *how*. He was to identify and make friends with some of the very wealthy students. He was to find out where they lived and what kind of businesses they owned. He was also to get into their homes, diagram the layouts, and identify what items of value they had, like cash, guns or jewelry.

"He even wants to know about their alarm systems, safes, and any other security measures; like dogs." Counter just sat there, in the over-stuffed leather chair ringing his hands and on the verge of tears. "I don't know what to do," said Counter. "I'm in a trap! If I don't get him the information he wants, he'll kill me and Sheila. If I give him wrong information, he'll kill us. I don't know what to do!"

"What about going to the police?" asked Banner.

"That's crazy!" snapped Jimmy Counter. "Kimbrel's nuts! That's the worst thing I could do."

"That's okay," said Banner; putting his hand on Counter's shoulder, trying to calm him down. "We'll figure something out."

He then looked at his watch. "I really have to get going, or I'm going to be late for class."

"I'll call you later," Caldwell said to Banner. "We can get together, if you're not chasing down some new headline story, and discuss this over coffee."

Banner gave a thumb up as he grabbed his books and headed out the door. But he was worried—with good reason. He then went to class, where he received all kind of accolades from his fellow students. Even the teacher complimented him on his headline story. After class, he headed off to work.

"If Jimmy does what Kimbrel wants," Banner said to himself, as he drove into the Times Union parking lot, "he'll be an accessory to burglary or worse." Banner knew that Kimbrel was capable of anything, including murder.

"Great story, James," Brince Thomas said to Banner as he stepped off the elevator.

"Thank you, sir," Banner replied; "and thank you for putting it on the front page. That's quite an honor."

"I only suggested it," Thomas modestly said. "The final decision was the publisher's. He also said he's coming by to see you today."

"What!" Banner said. "Mr. Grimily?"

"That's what he told me to tell you when he called my home this morning."

"Is that a good thing or bad thing?" asked Banner.

"I have no doubt that it will be a good thing," replied Thomas. Brince Thomas was smiling like a Cheshire cat.

Sean Franklin Grimily was a self-made multi-millionaire. He started off pushing a broom at the Florida Times union over thirty-five years ago, but Grimily had two basic faults, which turned out to be golden talents. He always spoke his mind and he was extremely thrifty. Many simply said that he was cheap. He had saved almost every penny he made. He either hitch-hiked to work or took public transportation. He did not even own a personal car until he became City Desk editor/manager. Even then he had a vehicle furnished by the paper.

The money that Grimily saved he reinvested into Florida Times Union Stock. When asked why he did that, his answer was always the same.

"I'll own this paper someday; and I want it to be financially solvent when I buy it!"

No one ever took him seriously, which only spurred his determination to accomplish that goal. Sean Grimily quickly went up through the ranks of the paper. Many said that the reason he got promoted so rapidly was his personality. Even Brince Thomas, who seemed very cold at that time to Jimmy Banner, once said that Grimily rose to the top so quickly because everybody loved to be around him. He was a gifted manager and an outstanding leader. He was also a man of his word.

"If he told you something," said Thomas, "he meant it, and he would never go back on his word."

"So, you're the young man whom our new Executive Editor has referred to as our 'Golden Child,'" said Sean Grimily.

Jimmy Banner was speechless.

"I'm very confused," Banner said, as his voice cracked. "I don't think I've ever spoken to Mr. Collingsworth. I honestly didn't realize he even knew I existed."

"I'm not talking about Frank Collingsworth," Grimily said with a smile. "I want to introduce you to our new Executive Managing Editor, Brince Thomas."

"This is unbelievable," Banner blurted out. "This isn't a joke. Is it?" Jimmy Banner immediately rushed to Brince Thomas, with his hand out, expecting to shake his hand. He thought he had over-stepped his boundaries when Thomas pushed Banner's hand aside. Thomas then smiled and immediately embraced Banner in his arms.

"This is fantastic news," Banner whispered to Thomas.

"It gets even better," Thomas whispered back, as he continued to embrace him.

"I also need for you to hand me your Press Identification." Grimily interrupted.

Banner looked surprised but did exactly what Mr. Grimily asked.

Grimily then looked at Thomas, and simply said, "Let me have your scissors, Mr. Executive Managing Editor."

"Yes, sir." Thomas answered, and then handed him a pair of scissors from the top of his desk.

The Publisher/Owner then began to slowly and methodically cut Banner's Press ID into small pieces. Banner looked on with both shock and confusion.

"I don't understand," he slowly said, as he looked towards Brince Thomas for answers.

Thomas continued smiling, as he nodded to his young star reporter. Once Grimily finished cutting up Banner's ID he turned and started to walk away. He then stopped and turned towards Thomas.

"I'm sure you can handle the rest, Mr. Executive Managing Editor," said Grimily

"I certainly can," smiled Thomas. "I sincerely want to thank you, again, Mr. Grimily, for allowing me to do this, especially now."

Grimily only nodded. "You both deserve this," he said as he shook Thomas' hand; and then shook Banner's, utterly confused, hand.

Thomas then reached into the top drawer of his desk and retrieved a brand-new Identification card. He then signed it; and handed it to Banner.

"Congratulations, Senior Reporter James Banner," said Thomas. "As my first official act as Executive Managing Editor, I'm promoting you to Senior Reporter and director of Major Events."

James Banner, at the age of twenty-two, was now the youngest Senior Reporter and youngest Director of Special Events, in the history of the Florida Times Union.

"I don't know what to say." Banner's voice started to crack, and his chest became tight; as he began to chock-up with emotion. The tears in his eyes welled up and then tumbled onto his cheeks. Brince Thomas walked over to him and put his arm around the visibly shaken new Senior Reporter. Grimily also walked over and shook Banner's hand, once again.

"You really do deserve this, son," said Grimily; "and what better way to be promoted Than by the man who recommended it." Grimily then took a step backwards and threw open his arms and shouted; "Now the two of you get out of here and go celebrate!"

A sudden burst of applause exploded, as the entire evening staff, who had gathered, unbeknownst to either Banner or Thomas, clapped with their approval of the promotions.

Banner who was still in a slight state of shock turned towards Brince Thomas and said, "I'll never be able to repay you."

"Just continue doing, what you've been doing," answered Thomas. "Take the day off, James; and take that new girlfriend of yours to dinner; on me." He then handed Banner a Hundred-dollar bill.

Banner immediately went to his desk telephone and called his girlfriend, Barbara Howard.

"I've been ordered by my boss to take you to dinner." Banner told Barbara.

"I don't understand," she said.

"I just got a promotion," he answered. "Mr. Thomas gave me a hundred dollars to celebrate."

"There's no way that we can spend a hundred dollars on dinner," Barbara responded. "Let's invite Jack and, his almost fiancé, Tammy, to join us."

"Great idea," Banner answered. "I'll call Jack right now."

The dinner consisted of four filet mignons and two bottles of imported French wine. It was a celebration like no other.

Six

After celebrating a great evening, Banner and Caldwell came crashing back to reality when hearing Vernon Kimbrel's name. "I was hoping that he was just a bad dream," Banner remarked to Caldwell. "So, what's the latest?"

"He showed up again last night at Jimmy's apartment." Caldwell's tone was one of deep concern. "I think that he's going to continue to intimidate him— or else just kill him."

"Do you really think that Kimbrel's capable of committing murder?" asked Banner.

"Absolutely," answered Jack. "I definitely know a sociopath, and Vernon Kimbrel is a hardened sociopath. I saw so many in the military. They join for the sole purpose of getting a chance to kill." Shaking his head, Caldwell bit his lip; he started to get emotional.

"When I was seventeen, I immediately signed up to go to Vietnam after high school, as an advisor." Caldwell's voice flattened into a monotone. "My sergeant was a lifer." Which meant that he was a career soldier. "He looked hard and was ten years younger than he appeared," continued Caldwell. "He never smiled and never did anything that didn't benefit him first. He was very cold and narcissistic. He acted like the whole conflict was about him. He loved to go into the jungle late at night. He would stay out almost all night, until the early hours of the morning."

Caldwell stopped and took a long drink of his beer, emptying the bottle. Banner went to the refrigerator and pulled out two more bottles of brew. One for him and another for Caldwell.

"Thanks, James," said Caldwell.

Banner smiled and nodded. "Please continue."

"Sergeant Drew Arroway, that's the name," continued Caldwell. "He would come into the basecamp from the jungle about three or four in the morning. He was always carrying a large burlap bag and a machete."

"What was he carrying?" asked Banner.

"I never really knew. I never actually saw inside of the bag." Caldwell answered. "He claimed that it was of his night-time ventures. Our Captain became concerned when some of the local villagers complained that their children were missing. So, he ordered him to open the bag." Caldwell stopped and took another swallow of his beer. "What he saw caused the Captain to order him to stop. He wanted to investigate.

"The top brass, however, knew that increased body counts looked good to Washington. So, they rescinded the Captain's order and removed him from command. Destroyed his career. Arroway, however, got promoted to Staff Sergeant; and was given the Silver Star for valor. He remained in Nam for another year."

"That's horrible," said Banner. "By the way, what did the Captain say was in the bag?"

"According to the rumors," answered Caldwell, "It was scalps, which Arroway, took as trophies. Some of them were children's scalps."

"My God," Banner yelled. "That guy was not human. He truly was an animal. What happened to him?"

"When he returned to the States," Caldwell answered, "after six months he was arrested and convicted in Fort Lewis, Washington, for killing five women in Seattle. It was estimated, however, that he was responsible for the deaths of thirteen women and children."

"That's unbelievable!" was all that Banner could say.

Taking a long gulp, Caldwell finished his second bottle of beer.

"What happened to that animal?"

"He was Court Marshalled, convicted, dishonorably discharged, given the death penalty and executed," answered Caldwell. "That, my friend, is a true serial killer. All the same characteristics I see in Vernon Kimbrel."

"We have to do something," said Banner.

"You're absolutely right," answered Caldwell. "And I think there's a way to get through this. It's going to be a little risky and dangerous; but I think it will work and get Vernon Kimbrel out of our lives for a long time—and hopefully, forever."

James then explained his plan. A plan which would involve Jennifer Cumming. Because of his position with the newspaper, Banner was able to find out that Jennifer Cumming was the daughter of Buck Lance, the former Chief of Police of the Jacksonville Police Department and now-present Undersheriff of the Jacksonville-Duval County Police Department. Buck Lance was second in command of the Department with direct control of the Patrol and Detective Divisions.

After agreeing that it could work, they also agreed that they would not tell Jimmy Counter that there even was a plan. It was critical that Counter not know anything in order to protect him—and by extension, the two of them.

Many things are predictable in life; some more so than others. There is absolutely no way that James Banner could have predicted that his plan would permanently alter the course of both his and Jack Caldwell's life forever.

"I'll do whatever you want me to do, except go to bed with Jack," Jennifer said with a smile. "Just tell me what you need."

Banner explained that they needed to talk, in private, with her father. They explained why; and told her why it had to be so secretive. They knew that Jennifer was beyond reproach, regarding her loyalty and love for them. Saving someone's life tends to do that.

"How about if I have him meet you in my office in the back of the student center. There is a back entrance, which few people know about. The University built it for me—because of the attempted robbery." She slightly chocked up.

Jack took her hand and held it with both of his. She kissed him lightly on the cheek.

"That would be great," said Banner. "Could he do it this Saturday?"

"How about three o'clock?" asked Jennifer. "He plays golf in the morning and I know he is not going to give that up for anything. He will also want to bring Major Johnny Hunt, whom is basically his right-hand man. I know daddy completely trusts him; and so, do I."

"Perfect," responded Banner. "Your trust, in him, is all we need."

"So, you feel sure you can set this up?" asked Jack.

"I guarantee it," Jennifer Cumming, confidently, responded. "They'll both be here, in my office, at three o'clock Saturday afternoon. If the two of you are early, I'll have some of my famous coffee brewing."

Jennifer Cumming was not kidding. Everyone who had ever tasted her coffee said that she should open her own coffee shop, or mass produce her coffee. They would always end with the same statement: "Whatever you decide to do, Jen, just let me know and I'll chip in to help finance you."

"I might hold you to that someday," Jennifer would reply.

Everyone would also ask, "What is your secret ingredient?"

Jennifer would always give the same answer, "My great grandma passed it down to my grandma and she passed it down to my mom, who passed it down to me. That's a four-generation secret; and I intend to keep it that way for four more generations."

It was 2:30 pm, then, on that Saturday afternoon, when Caldwell and Banner were comfortably sitting in Jennifer Cummings office, sipping, a cup of her four-generation secret ingredient coffee. It was delicious.

At exactly three o'clock there was a sharp knock at the door. Jennifer greeted her dad and Capt. Johnny Hunt with an embrace and a kiss.

"I already know him," Lance said, pointing to Banner; "But I don't know you, sir." He stuck out his hand to Jack.

"Jack Caldwell, sir. I'm Jimmy's roommate." He then shook both Lance's and Hunt's hands.

"Oh yes," said the Undersheriff. "Now I know who you are. My words of thank you mean nothing in comparison to the gift you gave me by saving my daughter's life two years ago." He then grabbed Caldwell's and Banner's hands and held them and let the tears well up in his eyes. "I don't care what it is you two wants. I can guarantee you that it will be done."

Johnny Hunt smiled, and once again, agreed with his boss. "That goes for me too, fellas," Hunt said.

"Thank you, Chief and Captain," said Banner. He then, abruptly and awkwardly, apologized. "I'm so sorry. I should have said Undersheriff and Major." His face reddened.

Both Hunt and Lance smiled. "Don't worry about it, son," said the Undersheriff, "We're just getting used to it ourselves. By the way, it's my understanding that you were the one who made that suggestion to Sheriff Parsons. Is that right?"

Jimmy Banner nodded and smiled. "The truth is, sir, that I told my boss, Brince Thomas, that I thought it would be a good idea, since he plays golf, with the Sheriff so often, I asked him to bring it up and see what he thought about it. He said he would do more than that, he would convince the Sheriff to do it; even if he had to lose the round to him."

The Undersheriff laughed out loud. "So, that's what Dale meant when he said he won me in a game of golf."

"Yes sir," Banner answered, laughing. "I'm sure that's exactly what he meant."

By this time both Jennifer and Caldwell were laughing too.

"We better calm down and get down to business," said Jennifer, holding back her laughter, "before the rest of my staff wonders what's going on in my normally quiet office."

"You're right, baby," said the Undersheriff.

Jennifer rolled her eyes, as she answered, "I'm not a baby, Daddy."

Lance responded, almost automatically, "You'll always be my baby and little girl. You know that."

Jennifer just smiled and kissed her daddy. "I know."

"Now what is it that I can do for you, James?" Lance said to Banner.

Banner and Caldwell explained the problem with Vernon Kimbrel. They then explained their plan of setting up Kimbrel with, what they called, "a false burglary".

"So, it was Kimbrel's idea to have Mr. Counter work for him to pay off his loan; and he would do this without pay?' asked Lance.

"That's correct," said Jack Caldwell, who was scheduled to teach 'Criminal Justice' at Terry Parker Senior High School.

"So, I guess you know where I'm going with this?" said Lance to Caldwell.

Caldwell nodded, "I think I do," said Caldwell. "He has already committed the crime of 'Involuntary Servitude' by forcing Jimmy Counter to work for him without compensation." Caldwell continued, "And since this was his idea he can't claim the 'affirmative defense' of 'entrapment.'"

"That's correct," said Lance, as he mimicked a soft clap. "You get a gold star.

How did you know that? Are you planning on becoming a lawyer?"

"No way!" Caldwell emphasized. He explained about his upcoming class.

"That's great," said Lance, while Hunt gave Caldwell a high-five. "That will make this a lot easier to explain," smiled lance. "Since it was Kimbrel's idea," the Undersheriff continued; "all you have to do is exactly what he asks. Just give us the name and address of the person, who meets Kimbrel's approval, and we'll do the rest."

Major Hunt and Jack Caldwell were vigorously taking notes, as Undersheriff Lance spoke.

"If you want," said Lance, "we could select the victim for you. Then we would feed you whatever information you need."

"I don't know," said Banner. "This is our first time at this. What do you think?"

"It's always best for you to have first-hand knowledge," Lance answered. "If you select the victim, and actually case the place, you would see things that we might not be able to describe to you. Do you understand what I'm trying to say?" asked Lance.

"I certainly do," said Banner.

"I completely understand," said Caldwell.

The undersheriff and Major Hunt gave Caldwell and Banner their private home and office numbers. They also assured them that they should have no trouble reaching one of them at any hour, day or night. In the rare situation, if they could not reach them, they should only leave a message on their home numbers.

"That's the best way to protect your identities," said Undersheriff Buck Lance.

Both James Banner and Jack Caldwell nodded in agreement. They all shook hands and hugged Jennifer before they departed.

SEVEN

THAT EVENING BOTH JACK CALDWELL AND JIMMY BANNER SPENT most of their time going over potential victims. The one name that seemed to fit all of Kimbrel's criteria was that of Joseph Solomon. He was extremely wealthy. The sole inheritor of a family fortune, he owned several businesses, including several jewelry stores, florist shops, two-gun stores and three bars. The common denominator for these businesses was the fact that they required Solomon to take huge amounts of cash from his businesses to a safe in his home.

Joseph Solomon was a classmate of Jimmy Counter and Jack Caldwell. He was the adopted only child of Henry and Mildred Solomon. He lived with his widowed mother in the exclusive community of Ortega, which is located between the St. John's river and the Ortega River.

The Solomon's estate consisted of a 16,380-square foot, living quarters; which was a four-story magnificent structure. It consisted of eight bedrooms, nine bathrooms, two master bedrooms and master bathrooms combined. One of the Master bed rooms was for Joseph; and the other was for his mother. There was also one ballroom, one large reception hall, an ultra-sized dining room, and a central kitchen. It also housed a 152,000-book library, a game room, two over-sized offices, an exercise room and Gym combination. There was also a heated pool in the basement. A twelve-car garage was attached to the main structure; and an Olympic sized swimming pool, with a pool-house, outside. A large eight-foot-high stone fence, made from

Italian marble, surrounded the entire living quarters; while a chain-link fence surrounded the 22-acre estate. The estate had a nine-hole golf course, a three thousand square-foot equipment house. Where all the tools were kept, to maintain the grounds. An 1,800 square foot Gardner's quarters was located next to the equipment house. A 5,400 square foot servant's quarters, which housed the estate manager, butler, estate driver, and three maids in six separate apartments. It was located just outside of the wall. A marble and tile tunnel ran from the servant's quarters to the main house; for quick and easy access. It truly was a mansion of the highest standards.

A holding of this magnitude came with a mighty heritage, of course. Henry Solomon, Joseph's father, was the only child of Anna and Isaac Solomon, both holocaust survivors rescued from Auschwitz; a Nazi death camp.

Shortly after coming to this country, Isaac and Anna Solomon opened a jewelry store on Riverside Drive. The store and jewelry business began to rapidly grow, because of the baby boomer era. The Solomon's strongly encouraged their only child, Henry, to attend college and study Business Administration, which he did. After Henry graduated from the University of Florida, in Gainesville, with a Master's in Business Administration; his father turned over the running of all of his businesses to him.

Henry married late in life. Some believed that he was too busy expanding his family businesses, and unable to have a social life. Early one afternoon both Joseph Solomon and his classmate Jimmy Counter had a little too much wine at lunch. At that time, Joseph unwittingly shared a family secret with Jimmy Counter. While he was in a totally inebriated state, Joseph made it known that his mother's real name was Mildred Van Dyke; and she was the daughter of a Nazi guard, who was assigned to Auschwitz.

Henry helped her to get her name changed from Van Dyke to Baker. At that time, he told her that it would protect her from any vengeful Auschwitz survivors or their families. Henry later admitted to her that he was afraid that his parents would cut him off from the family fortune if they found out her true heritage. Henry also admitted that was why he waited until his parents' death to finally marry her.

Mildred Solomon came to the end of her rope, however, when she accidentally found out, through some hospital receipts, that Henry had a vasectomy. When she asked about it, Henry went into a fit of rage. He said he couldn't believe that she was secretly checking on him. He went so far as to blurt out, "Your father must have been a member of the Gestapo for you to be able to secretly check on me!"

Mildred spat in his face and called him a coward and a liar, and stomped out of the house, and went to her sister's home in Murry Hill. Henry did everything he could to get her back; but he did it in a way that expounded upon his frugal and extremely thrifty nature. He would send her flowers, every day, from one of his floral shops. They were generally the fresh arrangements, that he was unable to sell that day. He also sent her different pieces of jewelry every week; and they were those pieces that had specific flaws, which he was unable to sell. He sent to her and her sister's family several bottles of wine each week; which he was having difficulty selling, in one of his liquor stores.

Henry Solomon had a sharp business sense; but an even sharper sense of how to be cheap. Seven months later she came back to him; when he promised that they would adopt any child of her choice. It was through that environment that Joseph came into the Solomon family.

Henry Solomon made an agreement with Joseph, at Joseph's Bar Mitzva when he was thirteen years old. He made Joseph promise that he would live a modest and thrifty life-style. He also made him promise that he would marry a Jewish woman, who maintained his thrifty life-style. Joseph knew that his father was directly attacking his mother's extravagant values. Henry told Joseph that the day he fulfilled this "agreement" he would then sign over ownership of his companies to Joseph. Joseph Solomon, reluctantly, promised that he would do as his father desired. The agreement, however, became null and void, when Henry had a massive heart attack three years later and died at the age of sixty-five. Mildred got drunk on the day of Henry's funeral. Some say it was because of her grief because of the loss of Henry. The majority, however, believed that she was celebrating the loss of Henry.

Ever since his father's death, Joseph, under the guidance of Mildred, lived an extremely extravagant life style. Once Henry was dead and buried, Mildred made a point of letting everyone know how cruel he was. Joseph even added to her drama by describing how he suffered both physical and emotional abuse at the hands of his adopted father. He went on to reinforce Mildred's claims of cruelty by stating that his father began, and spread, a despicable lie that Mildred was a Nazi collaborator. After hearing this, from Joseph, the outpouring of support for Mildred, from the family, gave her all the drama that she would ever need.

It was also through Mildred's unwitting encouragement, that Joseph became an alcoholic, at the young age of eighteen. Joseph's drink of choice was a bloody Mary; which contained equal amounts of Vodka and tomato juice. He always loved a piece of celery and a few drops of hot sauce added. He constantly said that "the true kick from a bloody Mary came from the hot sauce; and the celery would ease the pain."

That night, after Banner got off work, both he and Jack explained to Jimmy Counter that the home of Joseph Solomon should be the target of Kimbrel's burglary.

"That's a great idea," said Counter. "I can't thank you two enough for helping me through this." He, excitedly, said.

"Just remember us, when you get control of your dad's business and money," laughed Jack.

"You two will never have to worry about anything, ever again!" Counter said, hugging both at the same time.

"Okay," said Banner. "That's enough of the group hugs. Let's get down to business; and put this plan into action."

"James is right," agreed Caldwell. "First, Jimmy has to win over Joseph Solomon's trust and find out how much and where he keeps his money. We also must know when the most money would be in his safe, if that's where he hides the money."

"That's the easiest part." Counter said, to the surprise of both Caldwell and Banner.

"What do you mean?" asked Caldwell, in disbelief.

"Joe has a particular weakness, that only I know about." Counter said, almost arrogantly. "He is an alcoholic, who loves Vodka. He also loves bloody Mary's," Jimmy Counter smiled, knowing that both Caldwell and Banner were now hanging on his every word.

"Please continue," insisted Banner.

"The rest is simple," said Counter. "Once he's drunk; he spills his guts; but he only does it with me." Counter smiled, like a Cheshire Cat, once again. "He totally trusts me. I think it's because I was there for him in his darkest moments; and he has shared some dark family secrets with me; which I never revealed to anyone." Jimmy Counter then stood up, like a conquering hero. "And that gentlemen is why this part is going to be so easy."

Both Banner and Caldwell applauded, at the same time.

"Great job, Jimmy." Banner said, with Caldwell agreeing.

"Well, let's get the information, "said Caldwell; "and we'll go from there."

The next morning James Banner met with Major Johnny Hunt had outlined what they had done. Major Hunt was excited to hear the details and advised that he would pass it on to the Undersheriff, immediately.

Two weeks later Jimmy Counter came through with great success. He not only found out that Joseph Solomon kept his money in a Brink's 6000 electronic, and laser protected wall safe, with an outside monitor, in his master bed room; but he always kept a minimum of half a million dollars in the safe. He was also able to extract from Joseph Solomon, while he was in a completely drunken state, the fact he would have over one million dollars in the safe on any given weekend, while he waited to make his average deposit of $750,000.00 from his businesses.

Jimmy Counter admitted that he was only able to get six of the 12 digits of the combination to Joseph's safe.

"I honestly believe that, if I had another week," said Counter, "I could possibly get the remaining combination."

"Let me think about it," said Banner. "We don't want to spook him, by trying to get too greedy. After all, he is a very smart young man, drunk or not."

"I see what you're talking about," agreed Counter. "I'll let you guys make that decision, since you're on the outside looking in."

Eight

After meeting with Major Hunt and the undersheriff, it was decided to go ahead and set up the burglary for the coming weekend day of Sunday. Everyone agreed that it would be better to let the Sheriff and police to get the safe's combination from Joseph Solomon, when they explained to him what was happening. At that time they would tell Joseph to move his money to a safer location prior to 8:00 pm on Sunday. They also would arrange, with Solomon to have everyone, including the staff off the property.

Joseph Solomon, obviously, was very surprised when Undersheriff Lance, Major Hunt and Jimmy Counter showed up at his front door. Joseph looked at Jimmy and seemed very confused. He invited them in; at which time Buck Lance explained to him what was going to happen.

"How do you know this?" Joseph asked. At that time Joseph's mother entered the room.

"You can thank Jimmy, here," answered Major Hunt. "He was doing some work, at our request to make sure that you were not in any way involved in this."

"I understand," said Joseph. "Did I get a good report?" He asked, smiling.

"Of course, you did." Jimmy answered, also smiling.

Joseph and his mother had numerous questions; but they totally agreed to do whatever they told him to do. Both Mildred and Joseph thanked both Lance and Hunt for their work, and what they were doing to protect them.

The Solomons also knew that there had already been two home invasions in the Ortega community in the past six months. The father in one of the home invasions had been murdered, when he struggled with one of the invaders. The entire community had been gripped in fear, because of that senseless killing.

Lance assured them that they would be safe; and he and his officers would catch the perpetrators. Undersheriff Buck Lance had no way of knowing that Sunday would result in the worst nightmare he had ever known, and it would be one of the worst days of his career.

Jimmy Counter drove Vernon Kimbrel past the Solomon estate and showed him that it was exactly as he described.

"Since you know so much about the place, I might have you come with me," laughed Kimbrel.

"I hope you're kidding," said Counter in a broken and cracked voice depicting his overwhelming fear.

"Of course, I am!" snorted Kimbrel. "A coward like you wouldn't last five minutes doing my type of work."

This was one time that Jimmy Counter was glad that someone thought of him as a coward and a weakling. He glanced at Kimbrel and was filled with disgust and despair, when the realization hit him. He would be caught in the middle of this nightmare for an unknown amount of time. At first, he thought that a million-dollar heist would be enough for anyone to stop and retire from any type of job. That was not the case with Kimbrel. He was already talking about the next job that Counter would find for him; and how he hoped it was as good as, or better than this one.

"You know, Jimmy," said Kimbrel, "if you continue to find me jobs like this one I might even cut you in on some of the take." Then he laughed out loud. It was more of a graveling cackle; and he finally said, "in a couple of years."

Jimmy Counter started to get sick to his stomach.

"Is there anything else you want me to show you?" Counter asked in a sharp tone.

"No," answered Kimbrel. "I think I've seen enough. Take me back to my car. I need to rest before tomorrow night. I expect a big pay day." Once again, he spewed out his hideous laugh, and once again Counter felt like throwing up.

Sunday night finally came. Jimmy Counter was dreading it thinking that he would have to do this whole thing all over again in the next few days or weeks. Both Banner and Caldwell felt strangely excited and fearful at the same time. They all three had decided to spend the evening with their significant other to keep their minds off the incident which was about to take place.

Jimmy Counter was with Sheila at their home. James Banner was with his soon-to-be fiancé, Barbara Howard, at her apartment in Arlington. Jack Caldwell was with his fiancé, Tammy Green, at his and Banner's apartment. Both Banner and Caldwell were engaged to school teachers. James Banner met Barbara Howard while they both were working at a day camp; the summer before he started working for the Florida Times Union. She was starting a job teaching the sixth grade at Arlington Middle School that Fall.

Jack Caldwell met Tammy Green while he was a student teacher at Dupont Junior High School. He taught ninth grade Social Studies with Tammy, who was the primary teacher.

Both couples were having a double wedding on the same day in the same church, Arlington Baptist Church; there in Jacksonville, Florida. They were also being married at the exact same time, by the same minister, Dr. Emory Green. He was Tammy's uncle, and the pastor of Arlington Baptist Church.

They were to be married in a little over two weeks on August 4th. The phone rang at Caldwell and Banner's apartment at exactly 11:05 pm.

"Turn on Chanel Two. Right now, !!!" screamed Counter. "This is a nightmare! You're not going to believe this."

"What in the world," said Caldwell, who was just interrupted while in the middle of a romantic interlude with Tammy.

"I said turn on …"

"I know what you said, Jimmy," Caldwell said abruptly. "I'm trying to do it, so quit screaming,"

While Tammy found the channel, Jack called Banner at Barbara's Apartment.

They both then watched the Channel Two report in complete and total horror.

"Less than an hour ago," said the reporter; "There was a police shoot out in the exclusive Ortega community at the Solomon Mansion on Ortega Boulevard. Chanel Two news is presently sending reporters to the scene to find out exactly what happened." The reporter, Bill Redwood, was handed a note. I was just given an update," said Redwood. "It looks like we have tragic news," Redwood hesitated and swallowed hard. "Chanel two news has confirmed that a ranking sheriff's department deputy was killed in the shootout. Chanel two news has also confirmed that two suspects have been arrested at the scene. Law enforcement is not releasing any other information at this time, since they have not notified the next of kin of the deputy, who was killed in the line of duty."

Barbara Howards' phone rang again, and it was Jack, again.

"Okay. I'll let him know, Jack," said Barbara. "I know. We're all terrified and horrified over here; but I know that everything is going to be all right. God, bless you, Jack. Stay brave."

James walked over to Barbara and hugged her. "What did he say?"

"Your paper wants you to come in as soon as you can," Barbara said. "Jack said that Mr. Thomas was very apologetic, but he really needs you." Barbara looked deeply into James' eyes. She seemed both beautiful and uncanny at the same time.

"I honestly believe that you can read my mind, right now," said Banner, continuing to look into her eyes. He then kissed her deeply.

Barbara kissed him back. They held each other close; and gave each other strength.

"I know," said Barbara. "You do need to go to work; I can read your mind."

James smiled, slowly letting her go.

"Please be careful, James; and think about August 4th."

James Banner nodded, "That's all I think about," he said as he walked to his car.

When James Banner pulled into his reserved parking space at the Florida Times Union Office; he was met outside by Brince Thomas.

"I'm sorry I had to call you in, but you know these people better than any other reporter we have."

"Please, sir, don't apologize," James said. "I would do anything for you. You're also right, I do know these people and they are my friends."

Thomas leveled a deeply compassionate gaze at him.

As they both stepped on the elevator, Banner asked, "Do we know anything about the officer who was killed?"

"Yes," said Thomas. "I'm sorry to say this; but I think you know him, since you quoted him in one of your articles."

"My heart is breaking," said Banner. "Please, don't tell me it was Major Johnny Hunt!"

"I am so sorry," said Thomas. "I had no idea that you were close to him."

Once they stepped off the elevator, Thomas held on to Banner's arm, and looked directly at him. "If you can't do this," said Thomas; I fully understand. I promise that no one would hold it against you, if you were to walk out right now."

"There's no way that I'm going to do that. You know how I feel about you, personally, Mr. Executive Editor, and you know how much I respect you."

Thomas nodded.

"But I'm not going to be doing this for you, sir." James Banner's eyes began to well up. "I'm doing this for Johnny Hunt."

Brince Thomas smiled and said, "I understand."

"I'm also doing it for the over-time," laughed Banner to break the tension.

"You are a little ungrateful jerk," quipped Thomas. "Mr. Grimily did authorize me to pay you triple time, because you're my top reporter, and you're coming in on Sunday. I told him that I would decide, based upon your attitude."

Thomas put his arm around Banner and they both laughed and walked towards Brince Thomas' office. James Banner made numerous phone calls and talked to several different officers and the Sheriff and Undersheriff. Once he sifted through all of the information; and separated the facts from speculation; he began writing his story. It was 4:30 am when he finished. He couldn't believe that he had really held up the printing of a major newspaper for his one article.

"I actually stopped the presses," James Banner said to himself. "I hope it was worth waiting for."

It was probably one of the best stories that Banner had ever written. It not only covered the burglary and the stake-out by the newly formed Duval County/Jacksonville Police Departments; it also, described the accidental shooting of Major Johnny Hunt by one of his own officers.

"Although Major Hunt's death was an accident," Banner wrote, "both Vernon J. Kimbrel and William "Billy" Maxwell, who were arrested at the scene; would be charged with Felony Murder."

"This is probably the best piece you've ever written," said Thomas; when he sent Banner home that morning. "Don't bother to come in today," he laughed. "You can have the rest of the day off."

Banner only smiled and nodded. He then called his fiancé, Barbara, and told her he was going home to get some sleep; and he would see her that evening.

"You sound exhausted," Barbara said. "I read your article, and it was beautiful. I'm sure the Hunt family appreciated it. Now, go get some rest; and I'll fix you dinner tonight. Please remember how much I love you, James."

James Banner's heart always skipped a beat when Barbara told him how much she loved him. It often would boggle his mind as to what she saw in him. She was undoubtedly the most beautiful girl he had ever seen. She was also one of the smartest and kindest woman he had ever met. He loved her beyond his wildest dreams.

NINE

When James Banner got home, Jack was already up and dressed.

"I was on my way out to get my classes set up," Caldwell said. "I guess you've already put in a full day's work. By the way, that was a great story. I just finished reading it."

"Thanks," said James, halfheartedly. "How's Jimmy doing?"

"He's acting like he is losing his mind, as usual. I think he finally went to sleep," answered Caldwell. " He was calling me so many times; asking if I heard anything; that I finally had to take the phone off the hook about two this morning." Jack then looked at the phone in the middle of the coffee table. "I put it back on, about an hour ago. I'm sure he's asleep, since he hasn't called anymore."

"Don't worry," said James. "I'll talk to him, after I wake up. Just call him, when you get a chance, and tell him that I'll explain everything to him this afternoon. Ask him not to call me, since I'm sleeping."

"I'll take care of it," said Caldwell. "Get some sleep. I'm sure Barbara is anxious to see you."

"I will," said Banner. "By the way, this evening, I'll be at Barbara's having dinner."

"Remember August 4th is coming quickly," Caldwell reminded him.

"It can't come quick enough for me," said Banner.

That morning all the News stations, both television and radio were quoting the Florida Times Union article by James Banner. He literally became an overnight celebrity. He had more insight into the incident than any other news source could obtain. When reporters asked the Executive Editor and General Manager of the Times Union, Brince Thomas, "How was James Banner able to get so much information?" his simple reply was, "Because he is an honest and really good reporter."

"Do you remember when we first met?" Barbara asked James, as she brought the London broil to the table.

"I do remember how much I love your London broil," Banner said, with a huge smile on his face. "Of course, I remember when we first met at Happy Acres Day Camp."

"Do you also remember how many of the counselors you dated before you finally asked me out?"

James knew where this was going. In fact, he was surprised that she waited so long to ask it. He even helped her to take the question to its very limit. "I also remember that you were the very last one of the female counselors, except for Mrs. Scarborough, who was 58; and Mrs. Kitterman, who was 43."

"Then you know what I'm asking," said Barbara.

"Of course," he answered. "You really want to know why I asked you out last; and why I asked you to marry me on our second date."

"That's exactly right!" she said with a smile of victory on her face. She didn't realize that James Banner had almost a year to ponder this question.

"You forgot to mention, my precious angel," he said, "that I asked each one of those girls out only once; but you were the only one that I asked out twice."

"Whoop de doo," she said sarcastically. "What is that supposed to mean."

"It means," he answered, "that I was not looking for just a date. I was looking for a person with whom I could share the rest of my life. I knew to the very fiber of my being that you would be that person, after our first date. That is why I asked you to marry me on our second date."

Barbara's face turned bright red; and tears ran down her cheeks.

James immediately took her into his arms, with her sitting on his lap. He then kissed her gently, but deeply. They let every emotion flow through them, as they passionately held on to each other. James then stood up and carried her in his arms to the nearest sofa, without ever breaking their kiss. They sat on the sofa with her still on his lap. They continued kissing, until their passion became white hot.

"I wish that I had never agreed to wait until we were married" he said, sweat covered his body and a lust-filled desire engulfed him.

"It will make all of this so much sweeter," she said. Her heart was pounding with desire; and her senses were becoming numb. "I'm tingling all over," she said to herself. "I've never felt anything like this before. He must be the man God made for me." She thought; and she smiled.

They finally, reluctantly, separated and were breathing heavily to catch their breath.

Barbara leaned over and kissed her future husband on the cheek. "Let's have the dinner, that I specially made for you," she said. "Then, if you need to, you can take a shower."

He looked into her beautiful green eyes and smiled. "How much longer before August 4th?" he asked.

She laughed and flipped her gorgeous brown hair back over her right ear. She then punched him gently on the right shoulder. "You're like every man. You only think of one thing."

"You're right," he said; "and like every man I get hungry, so let's eat."

They kissed gently, being careful not to get all excited again, and sat down to eat the, still warm, London Broil. Throughout the meal, they both could think of little else than their upcoming wedding. They then went into the living room and sat on the sofa. Barbara fixed some popcorn and some soft drinks; and they enjoyed watching the various shows on television. Barbara then stretched out on the sofa and laid her head on James' lap, and gently fell asleep.

It was almost 11:30 pm when James picked her up, very gently, and carried her to bed. He would let her lay there with her halter and shorts, and only removed her tennis shoes and socks. He then set the clock for 6:00 am, since tomorrow was a school day, and she was teaching.

James deeply respected Barbara and he wanted their upcoming marriage to be perfect. Ever since they accepted Christ as their living Savior, through the guidance of Tiffany's uncle, Rev. Emory Green, they both turned their marriage and their lives over to the Lord; and they had complete peace. Even during the Vernon Kimbrel chaos; and the death of Major Johnny Hunt; they felt peace in the knowledge that God was in control. A peace that passes all human understanding.

TEN

AUGUST 4TH, THE CHOSEN DAY FOR BOTH JACK AND JAMES WEDDINGS, was a day filled with both sunshine and joy. One of the attendees stated that it was like watching a love story in stereo. Another stated that you could almost hear God and His Angels rejoicing. Both Jack and Tiffany, as well as, James and Barbara knew that their marriages were made in heaven.

Both James Banner and Jack Caldwell went to the Virgin Islands on their respective honeymoons. Jack and Tiffany went to St. Marks; and James and Barbara went to St. Thomas. It was a honeymoon that they would remember for the rest of their lives. Just as beautiful and blissful as their honeymoons were; the tragedy that awaited them, however, was as despicable and horrific as anything they could have ever known.

Shortly after they returned home to Jacksonville, Jack and James were called to meet with the Sheriff and Undersheriff. It was then that they learned that James and Sheila Counter had been brutally murdered in their home.

"They were tortured in unthinkable ways," said Lance. "It was either revenge, or they were looking for information."

"Why?" asked Banner, in both anger and disgust.

"Mr. Counter was scheduled to be a primary witness against Vernon Kimbrel and Billy Maxwell," said Sheriff Dale Parsons. "The main theory we have now is that Kimbrel had them killed to keep him from testifying; and to find out who you were."

"Why would you believe they wanted to know our identity?" asked Banner.

"They did not need to torture him to keep him from testifying," said Undersheriff Lance. "They only needed to kill him. There is also something else." He said after pausing.

"What else?" asked Jack.

"They tried to kidnap Buck's daughter," said Parsons.

"Jennifer?" both Jack and James shouted out.

Buck Lance only nodded. "Two Jacksonville police officers and one university security officer responded to a suspicious person call. The university security officer got there just as they were attempting to grab Jennifer. The two police officers got there just after they shot and killed the university security officer."

The Undersheriff grimaced, as tears began to well up in his eyes. "That young man gave up his life to save my daughter," Lance said, with a cracked voice.

The Sheriff put his hand on Buck Lance's shoulder. "They both got away in a black GTO, without a tag. Jennifer was able to give us a good physical description of the two, which allowed us to put out a nationwide BOLO."

"Have they been caught?" asked Banner.

"Not yet," said Parsons, shaking his head. "But don't worry; they will be."

"So, what's happening with Kimbrel and Maxwell?" asked Caldwell.

"Their lawyer is a pretty decent guy," said Lance. "He doesn't want them to get away with Hunt's felony murder and the burglary of the Solomon's house; so, he talked them into accepting a plea deal. He has them convinced that we have a lot more evidence than just Counter's testimony."

"What's the Plea Deal?" asked Banner.

"They'll get twenty years to serve and an additional ten years on parole," said the Sheriff.

"They should get the death penalty," Caldwell said, clenching his fist.

"I agree," said Lance. "Right now, however, we must concentrate on protecting you and your wives, as well as, Jennifer and her family."

"What do you mean?" asked Banner. "I thought you said that he was going to prison for twenty years?"

"He is," said the Sheriff; "but Kimbrel is an animal. He isn't going to quit until you and your families are dead, as well as, Jennifer and her husband."

"I'm not questioning your judgement, Sheriff, "said Banner; "But the reporter in me wonders why you think he's after us?"

Sheriff Dale Parsons took a deep breath, and stood up, as if to make a big announcement. He then picked up two police reports. "Neither Undersheriff Lance nor I wanted to tell you this," he said.

He then took another deep breath and looked down at one of the reports. "There were several calls from neighbors about a black GTO being parked across the street from Barbara Banner's, the former Barbara Howard's, old apartment" the Sheriff said with a slight smile and looking at James. "The incident took place shortly after Counter's death. By the time the patrol cars got there the GTO was gone. The callers did give a tag number; but the tag was registered to a 1962 Cadillac which was registered to Vernon Kimbrel."

The Sheriff then sat back down and continued. "We also received a call that a 1963 Chevrolet Impala was parked across the street from Mr. Caldwell's apartment, where you both used to live; and the tag was registered to our murder victim, Jimmy Counter. The patrol cars, unfortunately, used lights and sirens to get to the scene, which alerted the suspicious person, who left before they arrived. On both occasions the drivers of the vehicles were only identified as middle-aged white males, who were wearing dark clothes. There was only one person in each vehicle. Kimbrel, of course had a perfect alibi, since he and Maxwell were still in Jail, awaiting trial. His only statement was that his 'tag must have been stolen, while he was in jail; and the police were unable to protect his property.'"

"That's why," said Lance, "we believe that he was not only after you; but also, your fiancés." Lance went on to say, "as well as my daughter and son-in-law."

"That means our wives aren't safe now, because we're here!" Caldwell blurted out.

"Calm down," said the Sheriff. "We have several undercover cars, watching your homes, and your wives, right now; and they'll stay there for as long as they're needed."

"We know that you are doing all you can to protect us; and we absolutely appreciate it," said Banner. "The only problem is that your resources are limited. We cannot expect you to have officers watching us twenty-four hours a day, and seven days a week." James then looked at Jack.

"Both Jack and I, with your help, can do something to protect our families," Banner continued. "I have an idea; but I need to talk about it with Jack, first."

"I understand," The Sheriff said. Lance also nodded. "We'll step outside and give you some time to talk things over. Whatever help you need from us, the Undersheriff and I give you our words that we will do it or find a way to do it."

"Thank you," said Jack as Parsons and Lance left the room.

"Jack," said Banner. "I think that the best way for us to protect our wives for us to become cops."

"What???" Jack said, loudly. "Have you lost your mind. We don't know anything about being cops."

"We can learn," James said, confidently. "We can go to the police academy."

"That would take weeks or months to finish." Said Caldwell. "It might even take a year for us to qualify to get in. In the meantime, we're sitting ducks for Kimbrel and his thugs."

"I agree," said Banner; "but, I think I know how to do this."

James Banner explained to Jack Caldwell his plan and Caldwell agreed. When Sheriff Parsons and Undersheriff Lance returned, they listened to Banner's plan. Immediately, they agreed to help.

James and Barbara and Jack and Tiffany, twenty-eight days later, left Jacksonville and moved to Atlanta, Georgia. The move began a brand-new chapter in all four of their lives. It would be a new beginning, in many ways and facets: physically, emotionally, and spiritually.

It was extremely difficult resigning from their jobs; but the Sheriff and Undersheriff had already explained why they had to resign to both the Florida Times Union and The Duval County School District. The paper, Sean Grimley; and the superintendent of schools, Ish Brandt, agreed to assist in every way possible.

Both Grimley and Brandt were personal friends with Herbert T. Jenkins, the Chief of Police of the Atlanta Police Department. Brince Thomas and Buck Lance were also close and personal friends with Clinton Chafin, the Superintendent of Detectives of the Atlanta Police Department. Lieutenant Bobby Moore, the newly promoted head of the APD Intelligence Division and Internal Affairs, was a very close friend and former college roommate of the late Major Johnny Hunt. Moore met both Caldwell and Banner, when they all attended Major Hunt's funeral.

It was as a result of all of the above connections and friendships that a significant part of Banner's plan was able to be met. They were able to complete the police academy in four weeks. Instead of ten. They did have to agree to attend weekends and stay late on certain days. They were certified in firearms at the beginning of their training; along with their wives ... This allowed them to carry their weapons, and gave their wives an extra level of protection, in the event that it was needed.

As their training came to an end; and they both were ready to go on patrol, Banner said to Caldwell. "I think this is bigger than us. So many things have come together at the same time. I don't think that this is all some big coincidence."

"Then what do you think it is?" Caldwell asked, in a very skeptical tone. "It has to be a coincidence; because, realistically, there's nothing else."

"Oh, yes there is!" Banner said, confidently.

"Then, what?"

"I believe it's God," said Banner. "I truly believe that this is all part of God's design for our lives."

"So now you're going to go 'Priest' on me," Caldwell laughed. "I thought God ended that chapter in your life, when He had you expelled from the Seminary. I really don't think he wants you to be a priest, James. I absolutely believe that Barbara would totally support me on this!"

They both laughed and embraced.

Eleven

Captain Hiram Masters hated both Caldwell and Banner. He hated them from the moment they joined the force; and his hatred continued into the present. No one, in the department, knew why Capt. Masters held such deep contempt for the two officers. It was believed, by most of the officers, that their close friendship to Capt. Johnny Schackelford and Bobby Moore, was the key factor.

They worked on the Morning Watch, under his command, for less than a year; and then they were assigned to the Special Operations Division, by order of Chief Herbert Jenkins, at the request of Superintendent Clinton Chafin. They were both assigned to Major Bobby Moore. Their assignment took place because of the intercession of Sean Franklin Grimley.

"I understand that you're going to be promoted next week," said Brince Thomas, in a telephone call to James Banner.

"What are you talking about, sir?"

"You're scheduled to be assigned to the Special Operations Division as a Plain Clothes Officer," said Thomas. "That's per Sean Grimley. He just had your Chief over for dinner and he took him out deep-sea fishing a few days ago."

"You're the best Investigative reporter that I know," Banner said with a smile. "What about Jack?"

"You're always looking out for your best friend," said Thomas. "He's getting promoted with you. The buzz and gossip around APD are that you two are presently assigned to the worst Captain in the

62

department; Some guy named Masters. Sean told Jenkins that you two are way too talented to waste on a bad Captain."

"Who is 'Sean'?" Banner asked.

"I can't believe you asked that question" said Thomas. "'Sean' is Mr. 'Sean' Grimley, the owner of the Florida Times Union."

Banner's jaw dropped. "Mr. Sean Grimley the Owner/Publisher of the paper. I'm sorry; but I never got that chummy with him to call him by his first name."

"I said the owner, not the Owner/Publisher," Thomas repeated with tongue in cheek.

"I'm sorry. I don't follow."

"I was appointed Publisher and General Manager, By Mr. Grimley, last month." Brince Thomas was grinning from ear to ear when he broke the news to his dear friend.

"You're not joking are you, Mr. Thomas?"

"I'm not joking," said Thomas. "That means that from now on you are to call me 'Mr. Publisher' or 'Mr. General Manager.'" Thomas' laughter was very contagious, and caused James Banner to join in.

"That's the best news I've had in a very long time," said Banner. "I can't wait to tell Jack. Congratulations, Sir. I mean, 'Mr. Publisher' and 'Mr. General Manager.'"

"I knew you would say that," quipped Thomas. "Have a great week, my dear friend."

As soon as he hung up the phone; James Banner immediately called Jack Caldwell and broke the news to him about their pending promotions; and reassignment.

Jack was equally ecstatic. "I can't wait until we get out from under that guy," Jack said, talking about Captain Masters. "I know that Tammy, and I'm sure Barbara, are going to be besides themselves to know that we'll be home on weekends and at a decent hour during the week."

James, however, cautioned Jack," don't get ahead of yourself, my friend. We will be working Special operations, which includes narcotics and intelligence. It also includes a myriad of other tasks."

At first, Chief Herbert T. Jenkins moved Capt. Hiram Masters to the Morning Watch, thinking that he would be the least harmful to the fewest number of officers. He admitted he was wrong when Major Bobby Moore explained to Jenkins how Masters interfered with Caldwell's attempt to get help during his pursuit of the two hit men in Cobb County. Jenkins immediately transferred Masters to the North Fulton County Precinct.

"Now he's out of my hair and he's Fulton County's problem," Jenkins said. "I'm telling you, Bobby," Jenkins looked directly at Moore, "that man is going to let his ego cause him to self-destruct."

Little did Chief Herbert Jenkins know that his prophecy would prove to be true in less than a month's time.

At that time, Fulton County, did not have a police force or a fire department. It contracted with the City of Atlanta for its Public Safety. All officers assigned to the Fulton County Division of the Atlanta Police Department were either assigned to the North Precinct or the South Precinct. Atlanta was paid the cost of providing the police service plus ten percent of that cost by the Fulton County tax payers. Many called it a "win-win" for both sides.

Hiram Masters, however, did not only have an ego problem; he was also very stupid. He did not realize that almost everyone assigned to Fulton County was there because Jenkins did not trust them, or he just plain did not like them. In Hiram Ethan Masters case, however, Chief Herbert Jenkins was totally correct. His ego was about to cause him to self-destruct.

Masters felt like he was among friends, which was the worst mistake he could make. His rank of Captain gave him the privilege of being the Precinct Commander. If he had handled the situation intelligently, he could have stayed in this very prestigious position until his retirement. Masters, however, let his arrogance and narcissism govern his actions. He decided to convince everyone that Chief Jenkins was "messing" with him because he was a threat to Jenkins.

"I know that a lot of powerful people want me to be the next chief," said Masters at a meeting of his command staff. "It's because they have lost confidence in Jenkins and his dumb policies." Masters said as he pounded his fist on the table. That pound was followed by a nearly inaudible click, as a hidden tape recorder was turned on. "I have no doubt that his tyrannical reign will end soon; as well as, all of his illegal activities. He is nothing but an criminal, with a chief's badge, who wants to get rid of all of us honest cops."

Masters then paused and waited to hear the overwhelming applause; and standing ovation, which never came. The only one who applauded; but quickly stopped, when no one joined him, was Sgt. A. K. Smith.

Captain Masters ignorance and his honest belief that everybody at North Precinct loved him, especially his own hand-picked command staff, caused Chief Jenkins phone to ring off the hook, the next morning.

It took Major Bobby Moore forty-seven minutes to get Jenkins to calm down. He even had to call in Superintendent Clinton Chafin to help in the critical mission: to keep Jenkins from getting in his car and driving up to North Precinct, and doing physical harm to Masters.

"I hate that man," Jenkins said to both Chafin and Moore. "If he were here right now, I'd break his neck."

"Herbert!" Chafin said with firmness. "You need to calm down, so that we can all think this through."

Jenkins threw up his arms and looked directly at Chafin. "You're right, Clint." He said as he took a deep breath. He then slowly returned to his desk. "Do you mind getting me a drink of water, Bobby?"

"Of course, Chief," Moore said, as he turned to the small refrigerator in the back of Jenkins office. He then pulled out a large bottle of cold water and poured some into a nearby plastic cup.

"Here you go, Sir." Moore handed Jenkins the cup.

"Thank you, son," Jenkins responded, as he continued to steady his breath. "Well what do you think I should do to Masters?" he asked Chafin and Moore. "Fire him?"

"No," said Chafin. "You should do something far worse than firing him." The superintendent then looked at both the chief and the major and laid out his plan for Hiram Masters.

Both Jenkins and Moore immediately agreed.

"I think it's absolutely brilliant," said Major Bobby Moore.

"But I don't want him to just read it in a bulletin," Jenkins said, "I want to see his face when I tell him." Jenkins then called out to his secretary, Gertrude Penny.

"Yes, Chief?" Gertrude asked.

Gertrude Penny had been the Chief's secretary as long as he had been chief; which was a little more that thirty-five years. Every year she claimed that this was her last year. Jenkins, who was a genius at keeping employees he liked, would give her a raise at the end of the year. Gertrude knew that she would have to complete the entire year for the raise to be used in calculating her pension. So, she stayed one more year.

"I need you to contact Captain Masters at The Fulton County North Precinct," Jenkins said to Gertrude, "and tell him that I need to see him as soon as possible."

"Right away." Gertrude turned to leave.

"Oh, Gertrude," the Chief said, stopping her. "If he asks if he's in trouble, just say no you're not in trouble. In fact, it's something good."

Gertrude smiled and nodded; and left the room.

Capt. Masters did just as Jenkins expected.

"Why does he want to see me?" Masters asked. "What does he think I did wrong?"

"No, it's not that," Gertrude responded, as the chief directed. "I think it's something good."

"Well, thank you, Gertrude," Masters replied. "This is the first time, in a long time, that I'm looking forward to coming to his office."

Captain Masters made the trip from the North Precinct, on Sandy Springs Place and Roswell Road to Atlanta Police Department Headquarters, on Decatur Street, in downtown Atlanta in 34 minutes. It was obvious that he used the blue and red lights in his grille; and his siren, in his unmarked car, because the trip would ordinarily take 50 minutes.

"You can tell the Chief that I'm here," Masters said with a big smile on his face.

"Just have a seat," Gertrude responded. "I'll let him know."

"Captain Masters is here, sir," Gertrude said on the direct line to the Chief. "Yes sir," she responded. She then called two other individuals at the Chief's request. Chief Jenkins wanted to see them, too.

"He'll be with you, shortly," she said to Masters.

Masters only nodded.

Three minutes later Chafin and newly appointed Superintendent of Patrol Operations Bobby Moore were standing in front of Gertrude's desk.

"Just go on in," she told the two. "He's expecting both of you."

Bobby Moore stepped back a step and briefly glanced at Masters, who was looking angry, frustrated and confused all at the same time. Bobby smiled and brushed his right shoulder, which displayed a silver eagle, indicating his new rank of Superintendent. As he stepped towards the Chief's office, he saw the Captain's face turn a bright red. He smiled once more.

"What going on, Gertrude?" Masters whispered. "I thought that this was supposed to be something good?" Sweat was pouring from his forehead, and his knees were literally shaking, and they would periodically knock together.

"Just relax, Captain," Gertrude responded. "I'm sure he'll call for you in a minute. Can I get you some coffee?" she asked.

"Yes, please," he said. "Just make it black."

Gertrude Penny got up and retrieved a Styrofoam cup and poured him a cup of black coffee.

"Thank you," he said, as he nervously took the cup.

TWELVE

AFTER NEARLY FORTY-FIVE MINUTES OF WAITING, MASTERS WAS becoming extremely agitated.

"He does know that I have to be back at North Precinct," Masters said. "I'm supposed to meet one of the County Commissioners in about 45 minutes," Masters lied as he looked at his watch.

One of the many reasons that Gertrude Penny was the highest paid secretary in the history of the Atlanta Police Department—and the main reasons she worked directly for the Chief of Police for so long—was her uncanny ability to handle the excuses and complaints of every police officer. This included Captain Hiram Ethan Masters.

The moment Masters said he had a meeting with a County Commissioner, Gertrude picked up her phone and opened her directory.

"Which one?" she calmly said as she dialed the phone.

Masters turned bright red, then pale white. His eyes were as big as saucers. His mouth began to quiver.

"Wanda, this is Gertrude. Captain Masters of North precinct told me that he has a meeting with one of the Commissioner's in about 45 minutes ... Hold on, Wanda. Captain, which Commissioner is it? I have the Executive Assistant of the Commissioners on the phone."

Masters took on the appearance of a zombie, blood draining from his face. His eyes began to look pink as some of the small vessels in his cornea began to burst from stress.

"Wanda, I'll call you back!" Gertrude said anxiously. "I think he's having a stroke." She hung up and dialed Grady Hospital directly as Masters doubled over and spilled coffee on his newly pressed uniform pants. She then yelled for the Chief.

"What is going on?" screamed Jenkins as he came flying out of his office, which Chafin and Moore behind him.

"I'm not sure," Gertrude answered, now bending over Masters. "It looked like he was having a stroke."

Gertrude's phone began to ring. "Chief Jenkins office, please hold." She looked back to the Chief. "Suddenly he became white as a sheet and looked like he was going to faint or was having a stroke. I called the paramedics from Grady. They should be here in a few minutes."

"Do you know what caused this?" asked Chafin.

"I'm not sure, Super," Gertrude said. "Let me answer this call, and I'll try to explain."

"Take your time," said Jenkins. "The paramedics are here."

"This is Chief Jenkins office. Thank you for your patience." Gertrude said. "Oh, hi Wanda. We had a bit of an emergency here; but I'll explain later." She then talked to Wanda Messina regarding Masters' meeting with the Commissioner for several minutes. "Thank you, Wanda. That explains a lot. I'll let the Captain, and the Chief know." She then politely hung up and waited while the paramedics arrived and treated Capt. Masters.

"The paramedics said he's going to be okay," said the newly-promoted Superintendent, after the paramedics finished and were cleaning up. "They said that he appeared to have something called an 'anxiety attack'."

"I think I know why," Gertrude Penny said.

"Well, let's let the paramedics finish up and step back into my office," Jenkins said. "You too, Gertrude."

As they went back into Jenkins' office, Gertrude explained Masters subterfuge.

"None of the Commissioners, of course, knew anything about such a meeting," she said.

"Is he so arrogant that he faked a meeting?" asked Moore.

"We're talking about a narcissist, who wanted you to hurry up and see you," Chafin said to the Chief.

Jenkins nodded. "You're exactly right, Clint." Jenkins then looked at his secretary. "I guess we could say that you're the best interrogator we have. You caught him in the middle of a lie. I should put you in Internal Affairs and get rid of both, Hines and Gaines."

"Just doing my job, Chief," smiled Gertrude.

"Go ahead and send him in," Jenkins said to his secretary. "I also want you to join us and take notes."

Like a professional politician, Jenkins stood up and offered his hand to Masters as he entered. Masters smiled, clasping the hand tightly—a bit too tightly, like a man scavenging for a lifeline. When Masters turned to shake hands with Chafin and Moore they acted like they were reading a report and did not see it. Jenkins then motioned for Masters to take a chair between Chafin and Moore. Which Masters, reluctantly, did.

"Well, Captain," Jenkins said, "do you have any idea as to why I wanted to see you today?"

"Well, I hope it's something good!" Masters replied, with an obviously conjured up smile.

"That depends on your point of view." The Chief then removed a tape recorder from his top drawer and pushed the play button.

As the recording of his staff meeting at North Precinct began to play, Masters turned jaundice and then started to turn white, again.

"Not again!!!" Superintendent Bobby Moore said, with disgust. "Doesn't your stupid drama ever get old?"

But Masters was breathing heavily, and his color changed back to red. He then rose to his feet. Moore and Chafin also stood up and grabbed Masters by the shoulders and pushed him back into his seat. Bobby Moore removed Masters' service revolver.

Masters resisted, twisting in the seat. "That's an illegal tape. It's a violation of my constitutional rights."

"And what right is that?" Jenkins calmly asked.

"My right of privacy and my right of freedom of speech!"

"You need to calm down," Jenkins spoke very softly. "The only 'speech' you have made, at least so far, is 'Good Morning, command staff.'"

Captain Hiram Masters had to endure the repeat of the staff meeting. He kept fidgeting with his uniform hat on his lap. He also was constantly rubbing his nose and his eyes. At one-point Bobby Moore touched Masters' hand to calm him down.

"Get your filthy hands off me," Masters snapped.

Moore simply smiled and pulled his hand back. If a look could cause total annihilation, Masters look at the newly promoted Superintendent would have vaporized him.

Masters' eyes further reddened as he tightly began to gnash his teeth together. The recorder had him saying, "I know that a lot of powerful people want me to be the next chief. It's because they have lost confidence in Jenkins and his dumb policies." His eyes became a bright red, as he twisted his hat, as his voice rang out: "I have no doubt that his tyrannical reign will end soon, as well as all of his illegal activities. He is nothing but an illegitimate individual, who wants to get rid of all of us honest cops."

Captain Hiram Ethan Masters, soon after, became the first person in the history of the Atlanta Police Department to "throw-up" in the office of the Chief of Police. As he was puking, he fell forward and hit his forehead and nose on the newly cleaned carpet in front of the Chief's desk. To add even more disgrace to himself, Masters puked again, but mainly on himself.

"I can't believe you did that," Jenkins yelled at Masters. He then reached into his left desk drawer and pulled out a small glass bulb of smelling salts, wrapped in cotton. He handed it to Bobby Moore.

Bobby nodded, in acknowledgement, and crushed the bulb which contained the smelling salts. He then lifted Masters' head by the hair, while it was still face-down in his vomit, and pressed the cotton, which was now soaked in smelling salts, against Masters' nose.

"What in the world," Hiram Masters screamed, as he abruptly awoke, and instinctively put his vomit-covered hand to his nose. As the pungent smell of his putrid vomit invaded his nostrils Masters screamed, again.

"Clint," Jenkins said, "have somebody take him to the restroom; and hand him my new order and directive."

Chafin nodded. "Come with me, Captain," he said directing Masters to the Chief's private bathroom. He then called Lieutenant Jerod Spence, the commander of SWAT, When Spence arrived, he explained to him the details. He then handed him The Daily Bulletin, which contained Jenkins latest order and directive. Chafin told Spence what to do with Masters, after Masters read the Bulletin.

"Don't worry Super, I'll take care of it," Spence replied, and saluted.

"We're inside, Jerod," Chafin remarked. "You don't have to salute me."

Spence's answer caused everyone to stop what they were doing and take notice.

"I'm not doing it because I have to," Spence said. "I'm doing it because of my deep respect for each of you."

Superintendent Clinton Chafin swallowed hard. He then lifted his right hand and returned the salute.

Spence, with his salute still in place, turned towards Chief Jenkins and Superintendent Bobby Moore. Both solemnly returned his salute.

They all three thanked the Lieutenant.

Chief Jenkins then abruptly broke the solemnness of the moment. He said, "Bobby, can you, please have somebody come up here to fumigate and clean up this mess."

"No problem, Chief." Moore responded with a smile on his face.

"Thank you both," Jenkins said to the two Superintendents. He then left his office and stepped into Gertrude Penny's office.

"Gertrude," Jenkins said to his secretary, "as soon as the Superintendents finish their duties; bring them with you into the hall way and we can all go to lunch, since today's events caused us to miss it."

Gertrude Penny smiled as she responded, "Of course, Chief."
Jenkins then left her office and stepped out into the hallway and
walked towards the elevators.

THIRTEEN

LESS THAN TEN MINUTES LATER GERTRUDE MET CHIEF JENKINS, who was seated on a bench in front of the elevators.

Gertrude joined him. "I need to say something Chief."

"Of course," said Jenkins. "What's the matter?"

"I feel like part of this is my fault," Gertrude said with a tear in her eye. "I think I'm the one who caused Capt. Masters to nearly have a stroke when I caught him in that lie about meeting with the Commissioner."

Herbert Jenkins looked directly into her eyes and stood up. He the raised her to her feet, never letting go of her hands.

"Yes, it is; and yes, you did," Jenkins said, with a big smile on his face, "and for that I'm going to give you another raise. You were brilliant in the way you checked on Masters' excuse. I'm so proud of you, Gertrude." He then did the most shocking thing of all. He hugged Gertrude Penny.

Gertrude, still feeling a little upset with herself for getting Capt. Masters into so much trouble, returned his hug with just one arm.

"I'm so sorry," Jenkins said with a red face and sheepish grin.

Gertrude Penny stood on her toes and kissed Jenkins on the cheek. "Don't be. You're very dear to me; and I'm glad you did."

It appeared as if someone had flipped a switch in Chief Herbert Jenkins. His face lit up. He straightened his posture and was grinning like a Cheshire cat. At that time both Chafin and Moore stepped into the Hallway. Jenkins pressed the down button for the elevator.

When the elevator arrived, Jenkins offered his arm to Gertrude; and she enthusiastically took it. "Boys, and Lady," Jenkins said, "Lunch is on me!"

"What's going on?" Moore whispered to Chafin.

"You're supposed to oversee Intelligence," Chafin whispered. "It doesn't take much intelligence to figure this out."

Bobby Moore smiled and nodded.

Herbert Jenkins had never bought anyone lunch since the day he had been appointed Chief of Police. His employees would always insist on paying for his meal. If he were taking guests or visitors out for lunch he would let the city pay for it, by way of reimbursement.

This was the first time since his wife died of cancer that Gertrude Penny had seen him genuinely happy. It was also the first time, since her husband passed away, that she felt genuinely happy. She pulled his arm, a little closer to her. He smiled once again. When they stepped outside and started to walk to his reserved parking spot, he turned towards his two superintendents. "Why don't you two follow me?"

"Yes, sir," they both smiled.

"Nicolai's Roof," Chief Jenkins said to the shocked driver.

Rather than having the entire police department starting rumors about his chief, Captain Robert Reynolds, his driver, simply radioed to the two superintendents to just follow him.

Nicolai's Roof was the most elegant and most expensive restaurant in all Metropolitan Atlanta. Gertrude almost fainted when the Chief of Police held her door open and she overheard their destination. She felt like a queen, riding with her king, and their two knights following them.

Fourteen

Hiram Ethan Masters was a coward. His tough and mean facade was only a protection mechanism. He used it to hide his cowardice. When he finally got a lot of the vomit from his face and hair; and he wiped some of the blood from his carpet-bruised nose; he looked directly at Jerod Spence,

"Lieutenant," Masters said, in a tone that emphasized the fact that Spence was a subordinate; "find me some decent clothes!"

"I think you need to read this first, Captain," Spence said, biting his lip. He knew that he would no longer be calling Masters captain ever again.

Masters snatched the paper. "I don't care what this piece of paper says!" Masters' words were harsh and biting. "I'm still your Superior Officer and you're only a lieutenant. I'm ordering you to get me something decent to wear, or you'll be charged with insubordination! Now do you understand me,"

"Oh, yes," Spence said, looking directly at Masters and smiling. "I understand you; and my answer is still no. You're an arrogant jerk; and you deserve everything in this order."

Hiram Masters eyes became as big as saucers. He gasped and pulled his hand up to his chest in total disbelief of what the Lieutenant was saying.

"Listen to me, Lieutenant! You're suspended from duty, without pay, awaiting a hearing."

"Only the Chief of Police can do that." Spence said in a somewhat calm voice.

Total confusion, absolute fear and everything that happened thus far caused Hiram Masters to make the next statement.

"Chief Jenkins is not here," Masters said, nearly shouting. "since I'm in his office, I must be the acting Chief, so I'm suspending you without pay, until we have a hearing!"

There is little doubt that Lt. Jerod Spence, could have eventually convinced Hiram Masters to acknowledge the written orders of the Chief of Police; but he was very thankful when Superintendent Grady Tuggle, Director of Training and Personnel, opened the Chief's private bathroom door. Tuggle had stepped into the Chief's office to leave him a written message.

"What is going on here?" Tuggle asked in his nasal voice.

"Thank God, you're here, Superintendent," Masters yelled out. "This Lieutenant is being grossly insubordinate."

Tuggle had a confused and puzzled look on his face, until Spence quietly handed him Chief Jenkin's order.

"The Chief is not here Super," Lt. Spence said. "He and Superintendents Chafin and Moore, along with Mrs. Penny have all gone to lunch. They left me with the assignment of handing him this order; and so far, I have not been able to get him to read it."

"I understand," said Tuggle. "Masters read this bulletin! Now that's an order!" He then handed the Daily Bulletin to Hiram Masters.

Masters took it. When he first started to read it, he was not sure if his comprehension was correct. He rubbed his eyes when he read the words "demoted to the rank of Patrolman ..."

"This must be someone else," he said aloud. "Who does it say he's demoting to patrolman? This can't be right." He continued reading out loud. "Report to Captain John Schackelford tomorrow morning at 6:00 am. I can't," he said, fighting back the tears. "I don't have any patrolman's uniforms."

"You'll be able to go downstairs," Lt. Spence said, "when you finish completely reading the Chief's orders. See Sgt. Donnie James, in supplies, in the Quartermaster Warehouse and he'll give you some uniforms."

Tears were now freely falling from Patrolman Masters face. The orders of the Chief went on to say that Masters' demotion "would include a reduction in pay and benefits to that of a beginning Patrolman. He would be exempt from attending the academy but would not be exempt from performing the rigorous assignments expected of every Atlanta Patrol Officer. He would also be expected to complete Field Training Officer Evaluations in accordance with the standards of the Atlanta police Department."

Former Captain Masters pulled out his handkerchief and wiped his face. He then put it down to blow his nose. He then attempted to feign a heart attack.

"Don't even think about it," said Superintendent Tuggle, the director of training, who not only taught paramedics but also had two years of medical school.

He quickly gave up the idea and just made a few fake coughs. Hiram Ethan Masters honestly believed that this had been the worst day of his life. Little did he know that it was going to get much worse. Almost every single person that he was required to see had been severely hurt by Masters; and they wanted revenge.

Sgt. Donnie James had been suspended, without pay, by Masters on three different occasions for a total of thirty days. He finally appealed to Capt. Schackelford, who was the evening watch Captain at that time. John Schackelford, despite Masters strenuous objections, did succeed. Donnie James did so well on Schackleford's shift that he was promoted to Sergeant. Schackelford had a gift in his ability to observe and recognize an individual's talents. He made special note that Sgt. Donnie James knew and understood logistics. A few months after James' promotion, Captain Schackelford brought what he observed to the Chief's attention. Capt. Schackelford also had the unique talent of "timing". The department, at that time, was having a serious problem with supplies and distribution. Certain shifts were given supplies which were greatly disproportionate to other shifts. This was being done due to favoritism or flat out bribery. Then Lieutenant, Bobby Moore, was able to determine that it was bribery.

"The entire supply section of the department," Moore told the Chief, "is part of the bribery. It is systemic and goes from bottom to top. You need to clean out that entire section, before it corrupts the rest of the Police Department."

Jenkins agreed.

"What do you recommend I do?" The Chief asked.

"I, personally, think that Capt. Schackelford gave you the answer, when he told you about Sgt. Donnie James."

"That's perfect," said Jenkins, as he picked up the direct line to his secretary. "Gertrude, call Capt. Schackelford and ask him to come to my office, if he's not too busy; and to bring Sgt. Donnie James with him."

"I'll do it right now, Chief."

Donnie James still remembered that meeting that he and Capt. Schackelford had with the Chief. He was put in charge of the Supply Section. Chief Jenkins promised him that he would be promoted to Lieutenant, if he could show him that he deserved the promotion. Two months later Jenkins put out an order in the Daily Bulletin that Sgt. Donnie James would be promoted to the rank of Lieutenant, at the beginning of his shift on Monday, April 1st, 1974. The order went on to say that Lt. James would remain at his present assignment of Director of the Supply and Distribution Section.

Even though Donnie James had been so cruelly treated by Capt. Masters, James prayed for Masters and had made up his mind to forgive him. Masters, on the other hand, possessed a heart of stone. Evil was part of his DNA. Although he had a choice, he seemed to always choose the path that was most harmful to others, or most helpful to himself. He truly was the epitome of evil.

"I was asked by the Chief of Police to see you," Masters said, with a sinister smile on his face. "He said that you.ve been ordered to get me my new uniform. Is that correct?"

Donnie James knew what the order said; but chose not to humiliate Masters by telling him he interpreted the order incorrectly. He simply said, "I understand that I am supposed to give you a patrolman's uniform."

When he returned with the uniform, he laid it out on the counter. He also brought three others just like it.

"I'm giving you four uniforms, officer Masters ..." James said; but before he could finish Masters arrogance reared its ugly head.

"That's Cap ..." Masters stopped in mid-word.

"As I was saying, officer Masters," Donnie James continued; "I'm giving you four uniforms, instead of one, which I'm required to give you."

"What do you want, a gold star?" Masters was burning with anger and hatred.

"No; but a 'thank you' would be nice," said James.

"How about a dunce hat?" Masters said, laughing; "and one for your mother," He continued laughing.

Sgt. Donnie James could not take it anymore. This man was too filled with hatred, anger and the desire for revenge. James stopped filling out the unsigned forms which showed that he had distributed the uniforms to Patrolman Masters. He then pulled the roll-top door down to the counter and locked it. He then locked the main door to the supply warehouse. He went to his office, while Patrolman Hiram Masters stood there screaming obscenities at him and the top brass. Soon-to-be Lieutenant Donnie James then called Superintendent Booby Moore, who was about to leave for the day; and explained what took place.

"I'll be right down," Moore said. "I'm so sorry, Donnie, that you had to deal with this.""

"Don't you dare apologize, Sir." Donnie emphatically said. "You and Captain Schackelford are true examples of what a leader should be. I pray that someday I'll be half as good as you. Hiram Masters is evil. He's standing in front of the Quartermaster Warehouse, screaming out every known profanity, and stomping his feet like a spoiled brat."

"I'll take care of this, Donnie." Moore smiled and hung up the phone; and made a phone call to Lt. Jerod Spence. He then headed down to the Quartermaster Warehouse.

Hiram Ethan Masters was still in front of the locked door and locked counter of the Quartermaster Warehouse screaming every possible vile curse word that could be imagined. He was no longer standing, he was now sitting on the concrete floor. He was also pounding his hands and feet and flailing like a baby who was in the throes of a tantrum.

The Superintendent of Patrol and Operations looked, in total disbelief, at the bizarre scene which was happening before him. Lt. Jerod Spence, at the request of Bobby Moore, was filming the entire activity of Hiram Masters. After a few minutes, Bobby Moore walked up and touched Masters shoulder and told him to look at the camera. Masters paused long enough to see that someone was filming him. He briefly stopped, and his face appeared to be somewhat shocked. His eyes were filled with fear. He then looked directly into the camera. His facial appearance changed from shock to satanic. His eyes were no longer filled with fear; they looked diabolical and were filled with evil.

Lt. Spence looked on in total disbelief "He looks like he's possessed!!!" Jerod Spence was a combat hardened, Vietnam veteran, and a war-hero. He was also a highly-decorated soldier and police officer, who was now the Commander of the Special Weapons And Tactics Unit (SWAT). He had seen almost every type of heinous and horrific activity. He was a man who did not scare easily. Hiram Masters appearance, that day, frightened him.

Bobby Moore signaled Lt. Spence to stop filming. He then told him to put the film in to be developed; and he could go home.

"Thank you, Jerod," Moore said. "You're a good man and a fine Lieutenant."

Spence saluted and returned to his office.

"You're not a fine Lieutenant." Masters blurted out. "You're nothing but a "yes man". You'll do anything to compromise your values. in order to get a promotion

Jerod Spence was too far away to hear Masters vile talk.

Suddenly the quite soft-spoken, rarely upset, superintendent of police patrol and operations grabbed Hiram Masters by the nose, squeezed, and jerked his head backwards. Masters instinctively opened his mouth, since he could not breathe through his nose. At that moment, Bobby Moore told Hiram Masters that his biggest problem was exactly what he was using to breathe. His mouth. Masters did two basic things at that time. He acknowledged what Moore was saying; and he began to cry. Moore noticed that tears were flowing from his eyes and mucus was dripping from his nostrils. This was proof to superintendent Moore that he had somehow gotten through to Hiram Masters.

"Now listen to me," Moore said calmly. "Right now, you've been busted to patrolman. You've already been caught in several lies by the Chief's secretary. You're being moved from a very cushy assignment, which most men would kill to have. You're losing two-thirds of your pay. You've been assigned to work for your number one arch enemy, who can do whatever he wants with you. You also must call your wife at home to come and get you, because you longer have the car, which you drove here. If that isn't humiliating enough, you've been stripped of your badge, gun, captain's bars, identification card, and you're wearing a uniform that's covered in digested food, sweat, blood, dirt and tears. You now must plead with people that you have deliberately hurt, most of your career. You have to do this just to get the basic equipment you need to work, by tomorrow morning at 6:00 am. At that time, your humiliation, disgrace, and degradation will begin all over again; and continue for as long as you can possibly realize. Does that sum up your experience for today, former Captain Masters?" Moore paused long enough to let what he said sink into Master's mind.

Tears were now freely flowing down Masters' face. He nodded in agreement with Moore's summation

"This is your service revolver. I was supposed to give it to you today, after you signed Lt. Donnie James inventory sheet and receipt. I am also supposed to give you this Identification card and patrolman's badge."

The Superintendent of Patrol and Operations then looked over at the locked Warehouse and said, "You can come out now Donnie. I think he's ready now."

Donnie James came out of the warehouse and walked towards them. He took Masters by the hand and helped him up. He had to cover his nose with his handkerchief, because of Masters' stench. It almost caused the soon-to-be Lieutenant to pass out.

"Thank you, Superintendent," Donnie said. "I'll take it from here; and he'll be ready by 6:00 am tomorrow."

"I know you'll take care of it, Donnie," Moore said, as he turned to leave.

Fifteen

Early that morning, Superintendent Bobby Moore left a message for Caldwell and Banner to come to his office. What could this mean? Generally, if a ranking supervisor wants to see someone, and it's not because they have done something wrong, they will use the phrase "if they're not too busy," or "if they have time." If the individual is in trouble, the term "ASAP" is used.

"Radio to 181 and 182."

"181 and 182. Go ahead radio," Caldwell answered, indicating that Banner was with him.

"Make a 10 G to Superintendent Moore," Radio said; and then: "If you're not too busy."

Less than three minutes later they were walking into Moore's office.

"You two must have been really close," Moore said, slightly amazed.

"We were on our way up here to both congratulate you. And thank you," Banner said. They both shook the newly promoted superintendent's hand.

"Thank you," he responded, as he shook their hands. "Now why do you want to thank me?"

"For clearing us in that matter involving Maxwell Knowles, the hit-man who tried to kill us." Caldwell said. "We also want to treat you to breakfast at the Lucky Street Grille."

"We also have a present for you, Sir," Banner said, as he held up a box, which was a little larger than a shoe box. It was gift wrapped in Christmas paper.

"I don't think I can ethically ..." Moore started to say.

"It will be fine," Caldwell said. "You and everybody else knows that my partner, the minister, is not going to do anything unethical."

Superintendent Moore nodded in agreement. "I'd love to go with you to breakfast," he said, "but before that I need to fill you in on some important information I got late last night."

Bobby Moore then told Banner and Caldwell about receiving a call from a former informant now working as a prostitute. She told him about a "client" who asked her if she could "hook him up" with a hit-man. He went on to tell her that he needed a couple of guys, who were working with the police, to be removed from that line of work. He told her that his name was Vic. She wasn't sure if he was talking about actual cops or informants. One thing was certain, however: Her description matched Vernon Kimbrel's. The initials VK on his over-sized belt-buckle and his dark horned-rim glasses were a give-away.

"Let's just think about it at breakfast," said Moore. "When we get back we can then discuss a strategy."

Caldwell and Banner agreed. They all gathered into the Superintendent's brand-new Crown Vic and headed to the Lucky Street Grille on Lucky Street, Caldwell carrying the present.

When they arrived at the Grille, they took a horseshoe shaped booth, where all three could sit with their backs against the wall. Banner deliberately sat on the right side of Moore and Caldwell sat on his left.

"If I didn't trust you two so much", Moore said, with a smile, "I'd demand that you sit across from me with your hands on the table at all times"

They both laughed. Then all three ordered their breakfasts.

"Would you please say the blessing, reverend," Moore asked Banner.

James Banner nodded. "I'd be honored."

After Banner completed his prayer, Caldwell lifted the wrapped present from the side of his seat. "This is for you, Sir."

The Superintendent knew that Caldwell and Banner were the reigning champions of practical jokers. No one was exempt from their pranks. They even sent the chief a Father's Day card from an unknown address with a picture of a Chinese soldier, who stated that he was his illegitimate son from World War 2 and wanted to reconnect. Jenkins immediately told Gertrude, "Get the cop and the minister up here, ASAP."

Gertrude smiled and did as she was told.

Both Caldwell and Banner were hailed by almost everyone at the Atlanta Police Department for the creativity of their pranks. Bobby Moore knew in his heart that this had to be a prank; and he was anxious to find out what it was. He was also cautious. He slowly began to peel away the Christmas wrapping. It was a shoe box. He slowly lifted the lid, until he could see what was inside. He looked panic.

"Go ahead, Super, take it out and let's see it," said Caldwell.

Bobby Moore looked around the morning breakfast crowd at Lucky Street Grille. The place was packed with every imaginable type of individuals. Everyone from prostitutes to drug addicts, alcoholics, business people, doctors, lawyers and even a few judges. Several Judges and lawyers had even come to his table to congratulate him on his promotion.

"If it's the last thing I do," Moore said while laughing, "I'm going to have you arrested, Jack!"

"What about him?" Caldwell asked, pointing to Banner.

"James is too moral and nice, to do something this audacious," Moore exclaimed, looking at the Kilo of Marijuana, which was wrapped in plastic wrap.

"Would you believe it was his idea?" Jack asked.

"Absolutely not!" said Moore. "This has Jack Caldwell written all over it. Now hang on to this and pray that we get out of this place without being mugged or busted," the Superintendent said, shoving the package under the table unto Caldwell's lap.

When they got back to the office, Moore told his two detectives to get back to the evidence room, where they got it. He also told them thank you for the breakfast and 'Present'. They all laughed, and both Caldwell and Banner started to leave.

"After you finish turning that back to evidence," Moore said. "I'll need you right back up here."

"That's right," said Banner. "We still need to discuss the Kimbrel hit-man thing."

"That and something else," said Moore. Before they could ask any questions, he simply said, "now go."

"What do you think the other thing is?" Banner asked; as they rode the elevator to the first floor.

"He's probably promoting us," Caldwell said. They both laughed.

After signing in the returned evidence, both Caldwell and Banner returned to Moore's office. He motioned for them to come in, while he was still on the phone.

"Yes sir," said Moore. "They're here now. I'll bring them both in." He then hung up the phone and motioned for them to follow him.

"Sir," said Caldwell; "if I may ask; what's this about?"

"No," answered Moore. "You may not ask. Just follow me." He then led them to the Chief's office.

"He's waiting for the three of you," Gertrude said. "Just go on in."

When they entered, Jenkins stood up and motioned for them to sit.

"This is either very good," thought Banner; "or very bad. He only stands up if he's really pissed or really happy."

They sat and sweat was forming on both of their brows.

"I suppose you're wondering why I called you in here," Jenkins said, in his usual unemotional tone. "Well, gentleman, at your Superintendent's suggestion, whom I hold in the highest regard, I'm going to do something I've never done before."

Caldwell and Banner both looked at Moore.

"Sir," Caldwell said to Moore; "The pot was only a joke!"

Moore smiled and turned red at the same time. "I'll explain later!"

"Maybe you shouldn't," the Chief answered with a smile. "I think I'm better off not knowing."

Bobby Moore smiled and nodded.

"I'm promoting the two of you," said Jenkins. "You'll be skipping the rank of Sergeant; and you'll be promoted to Lieutenants, effective immediately."

If a single look could tell a story, both Jack Caldwell's and James Banner's stunned appearance, spoke volumes. Their stunned appearances, however, became near catatonic when Gertrude Penny escorted Barbara Banner and Tammy Caldwell into the Chief's office.

"It was Bobby Moore's idea to have these ladies, under my authority, to swear you in and present you with your new Identification Cards and Badges," Jenkins said with an audible laugh. It was the first time, ever, that anyone in that room, except for Gertrude Penny, heard Herbert Jenkins laugh.

"I figured," said Superintendent Moore, "that these two ladies are the only ones, on the face of this earth, that you two would ever listen to and follow their orders."

The entire group burst out into laughter, including the department photographer, who had just entered. The only two, who still appeared to be in a trance were Caldwell and Banner. As the reality of what was happening began to sink in, their sweat was giving way to tears, which was welling up in their eyes.

Both Tammy and Barbara immediately rushed to their husbands and immediately embraced them.

Barbara Banner then pushed her husband away and held him at arm's length. She looked at him in the most loving way; and very softly said, "James, if you mess this up, I will personally see to it that your family jewels become useless for the next two years."

Everyone seemed stunned, until Tammy held Jack at arm's length and simply said "DITTO!"

History was made in that instance, when Chief Herbert Jenkins office burst into unbelievable laughter. It even caused the SWAT commander to call Gertrude Penny's office to see if everything was all right.

SIXTEEN

BOTH CALDWELL AND BANNER WERE ASSIGNED, AS CO-COMMANDERS, of the newly formed Metropolitan Atlanta Narcotics and Intelligence Task Force. It was so new, and so complex, that it had to be voted on and approved by the State Legislator. It also was signed by the Governor, who appointed the State Attorney General as oversight to the entire operation. Chief Herbert Jenkins, and/or his designee, would be the director of the task force. Their mission was two-fold:

1. Eliminate, by any legal means available, all narcotics sales and distribution throughout the 29-county Metropolitan Atlanta area of their jurisdiction.
2. To gather and utilize, by any legal means available, all intelligence information on any organized crime operations throughout the 29-county Metropolitan Atlanta area of their jurisdiction. For the purpose of bringing these Criminal Enterprises to justice.

The Co-commanders of the Task Force would answer directly to Chief Herbert Jenkins or his designee. Jenkins immediately appointed Superintendent Bobby Moore as his designee to direct the Metropolitan Atlanta Narcotics and Intelligence Task Force, in addition to his present responsibilities.

For the next eighteen months both Lieutenants Caldwell and Banner led the task force into making a record number of seizures and arrests. Their taskforce had seized, confiscated and condemned over twelve and a half million in cash, nearly 970 kilos of cocaine, fourteen tons of Marijuana, 320 kilograms of heroin, eighteen Kilos of PCP (Also Known As: Angel Dust), 281,000 tablets of Methaqualone (Quaaludes); 412 firearms, 153 automobiles, fifty-seven trucks, twelve airplanes, eight boats, three helicopters, nine RV's; and arrested 718 individuals. There were already 597 convictions from the 718 arrests. Ninety-nine of the remaining 121 suspects were entering pleas; and twenty-two were still awaiting trials.

The Taskforce was not only a complete success; it was touted as the very best in the country. No matter how successful a taskforce might be, however, unless it could totally destroy a drug operation and distribution; it did not seem to be successful in the eyes of its operational staff.

It was not until July of 1981, that the Metropolitan Atlanta Narcotics and Intelligence Task Force got its first true break, which came at an unbelievably high cost. It was a cost that no police department, much less a task force, was willing to pay. The small, low-crime community of Villa Rica, Georgia, paid with its own blood.

Roberto "Bobby" Cardinal was a man of God. He was also one of the top narcotics and intelligence officers that the city of Villa Rica had ever produced. Although he was newly promoted to Captain and placed in charge of the patrol and detective units of the Villa Rica Police Department; he begged the chief to allow him to be assigned to the Task Force. Chief Billy Baker, a former Lieutenant with the Fulton County Police Department; and now newly appointed Chief of the Villa Rica Police, told Bobby that he would ask the Mayor.

Mayor Douglas Crawford, agreed to the assignment, if the Task Force was willing to share some its seized revenues with Villa Rica. The Co-Commanders of the Metropolitan Atlanta Narcotics and Intelligence Task Force agreed to the Mayor's terms. They then entered into an ongoing contract with the City of Villa Rica. Lieutenants Jim Banner and Jack Caldwell, as well as Superintendent Bobby Moore, and Chief Herbert Jenkins were so impressed with Roberto Cardinal that they agreed to provide him with a take-home vehicle, all of his insurance (Medical and Life) costs, his pension costs, promotional pay, overtime pay, and any per-diem expenses; as long as the City of Villa Rica was willing to pay his base salary. They literally made him an "offer that he could not refuse."

The revenue and drugs that Bobby Cardinal was responsible for seizing and the arrests, which he made, was worth 100 times the cost of his services. Mayor Doug Crawford once described Bobby Cardinal's talent as that of "a hound dog, who could smell illegal narcotics, even if it drove past him at 90 miles an hour."

Roberto Cardinal was a Lieutenant with the Military Police of the United States Army. He served in that capacity for three years. The last year of his tour he was assigned as the commander of a Military Police Detachment in Cam Rahn Bay, Vietnam. He earned one bronze star and two silver crosses for his outstanding work in stopping narcotics traffic in that region. There were two soldiers dying from an overdose of heroin every day at the military bases of Cam Rahn Bay and Nah Trang. Jim Banner was a CID agent assigned to Cam Rahn Bay and worked with 1st Lieutenant Roberto Cardinal. Banner primarily worked undercover under the guise of being a deserter, who lived in the village of Su Chin, which was located just outside the military base of Cam Rahn Bay. He would arrange for drug transactions with the Viet Cong. The Viet Cong would provide several kilos of heroin, which they said was cocaine, for "Green Backs", which were actual U.S. Dollars. The U.S. Dollars were worth more to the Viet Cong than their own currency. For $1,000.00 U.S. Dollars (Green Backs) Banner could purchase two Kilos of Heroin. Banner worked undercover with a South Vietnamese National Police Captain named Nyguyen Diep. Capt. Diep would identify the Viet Cong who would sell the drugs to him and Banner, in order to arrest them at a later date.

The size of the purchases would progressively increase, as would the number of Viet Cong delivering the drugs. Lt. Roberto Cardinal was able to obtain $30,000.00 in Green Backs for 60 kilos of Heroin, which laboratory tests had previously shown to be 98% pure. The sole purpose of a drug that pure was to murder those who used it. Their primary customers were United States soldiers.

Lt. Cardinal honestly believed that the only way he could have convinced the government to give him $30,000.00 to use for the operation was because of his father, who was Colonel Robert Cardinal, who was special advisor to General William Westmoreland. General Westmoreland was the commander of all military operations in Vietnam.

"I guess sometimes it's good to have some political clout," Bobby said jokingly to Banner.

"It's more than that," said Banner. "I'm convinced that God is totally on your side."

Cardinal Laughed. "He's on your side too, Jim. As long as we believe in His Son."

James Banner nodded in agreement.

The operation was considered a complete success. All 60 kilos, (252 pounds) of almost pure heroin, were seized. A total of 146 of the 147 Viet Cong and North Vietnamese soldiers, who delivered the heroin, were killed in an ambush. One ranking North Vietnamese officer was wounded, and taken alive, for intelligence purposes.

Roberto Cardinal was also a football hero. His years at the University of Alabama, under coach "Bear Bryant", made him a highly sought-after quarterback for the National Football League draft. After he received his bachelor's Degree, in Chemistry, he turned down all draft offers to join the military and serve his country in Vietnam. Despite his father's urgings, he decided not to make the military his career. He wanted to become a cop. He returned to his hometown of Villa Rica, Georgia; and joined the Villa Rica Police Department.

Roberto was given his name, because of his mother's desire to continue their Mexican heritage. Robert, her husband, who would do anything for the love of his life, enthusiastically agreed to name him Roberto. Col. Robert Cardinal met Consuela Gomez when he was a Captain, vacationing in Guadalajara, Mexico. He had an unfortunate accident, which turned out to be the best thing that ever happened to him, when he was stuck by a Mexican taxicab, which hit him while he was walking through an intersection. He was rushed to the

Universidad Autónoma de Guadalajara emergency medical center. It was primarily a teaching hospital. One of the doctors who was examining him was a beautiful young medical student, who was working in residence, named Consuela Gomez. She had dark black hair and stunning green eyes. Although she was only 5'2" tall she literally had an hour glass figure.

"Why are we honored with your visit?" she said, with a smile that could stop traffic in its tracks.

Robert just sat there, without speaking. He appeared to be in a trance. She shined a pencil light into his eyes; and switched from one eye to the next.

"Mr. Cardinale," she said in her exquisite Spanish accent.

"It's Card ... Cardin ... Cardinal," he finally said. "My name is Robert Cardinal." His voice cracked and sounded like it was strained.

"Is there something wrong with your throat?" she asked.

"You have got to be the most beautiful woman I have ever seen," he said. His face was flushed and red; and sweat was pouring from his brow.

She blushed and looked down. "Mr. Cardinal, you were involved in an accident. You were hit by a taxicab. I'm Dr. Gomez; and I'm your treating physician."

"Please call me Robert," he said. I'm okay. I do, however, want you to exam me, because I've never seen anyone as pretty as you."

That was Consuela Gomez's first encounter with Robert Cardinal. Eight months later they were married in the opulence of the Guadalajara Cathedral. It could best be described as a Fairy Tale Wedding. Something from the pages of Cinderella. It even included a carriage driven by four white horses, a driver and two footmen. It was described as "The Wedding of the Decade!" by **El Informador,** the local newspaper.

Robert and Consuela had a marriage like no other. They were deeply in love and they loved Jesus Christ, their Lord and Savior. He had a very successful military career and retired at the rank of Brigadier General. She was a successful Neurological Surgeon. They had two precious children, Delores and Roberto. Delores was in her third year of medical school at Mercer University, in Macon, Georgia. Roberto was working with the Metropolitan Atlanta Narcotics and Intelligence Task Force. Delores and her fiancé, Mark Pastel, a young plastic surgeon, were scheduled to be married in four months. Roberto and his new bride of one year, Jenny, were due to have their first child in less than a month.

It was on Sunday at 2:48 am, July 19th, 1981, that the then known world of the entire Cardinal family, at the hands of Vernon Kimbrel and members of his evil organization; would come to an end and test their faith to the very core of its foundation. It would also push the faith of James Banner, the minister, into the very abyss of total darkness.

SEVENTEEN

It was 12:56 am on that Sunday, July 19th, 1981, when the phone rang on Bobby Cardinal's night stand. He quickly answered it. He did not want it to awaken his wife, who was over eight months pregnant. She needed all the sleep she could get.

"Hello" he said in a very groggy voice. He also, simultaneously, hit the record button on the recorder attached to his phone. He'd done this since he joined the task force.

"I'm sorry, man," the person on the other end said. "Did I wake you?"

"Of course, you did," Bobby answered. "It's almost one in the morning, who is this?"

"You know who it is. It's Hercules."

Hercules Maxwell was one of Bobby Cardinal's best informants. Bobby had personally bailed him out of jail on several occasions. He was an alcoholic, who had found the Lord and was trying to get his life straight. Roberto Cardinal first met Hercules when he was just starting with the Villa Rica Police Department. Bobby responded to a call of a bar fight on the Southside of Villa Rica. It was one of the city's "high-crime" areas.

To the citizens of Villa Rica, "High-Crimes" consisted of drunk and disorderly, barfights, minor thefts, and occasionally, an auto-theft. This time there were three rednecks harassing and threatening a young black student and his wife.

The couple had accidentally come into the bar, which was

96

frequented by "red necks", to ask for directions. They quickly realized their mistake and started to leave. The three confronted them, however—asking why they were leaving so soon and accusing them of not liking white people. At that point, the owner of the bar called the police.

Hercules Maxwell entered less than thirty seconds before Bobby got there. Although Hercules was a black male in a primarily all-white bar, he was a frequent customer. Everyone seemed to respect Hercules Maxwell. The fact that he was 6' 10" tall, and weighed almost 380 pounds, had a lot to do with that respect.

When Hercules entered, he saw that one of the red-necks had broken a bottle of beer and was getting ready to stab the black male in the face. It was then that Patrolman Roberto Cardinal arrived. Cardinal confronted them and ordered them to move away from the couple. They simply laughed out loud.

"Do you think you're man enough to make us," Shouted an unshaven, stringy haired, muscular, white male. "That badge of yours don't mean anything to us!" He sneered.

Bobby moved in closer and put his hand on his revolver. "You don't want to make this any worse than what it is."

"Oh, yes we do!" said the loudmouthed muscular one. He then pulled out a switchblade and held it by his side.

Hercules Maxwell did not have an ounce of fat on him. He was massive. He had just gotten off from work. He worked for a concrete company and loaded 200-pound bags of concrete, on transport trucks, six days a week. He was built like a black bulldozer. Just one of his black arms was bigger than most people's thighs. Hercules moved around to the rear of the three red-necks and noticed that two of them had revolvers tucked in the back pockets of their faded blue overalls.

"Why don't y'all just listen to the officer," Hercules said in his slow southern drawl.

"Who the ...?" the stringy haired one started to say, as he turned to look at Hercules. He suddenly stopped in mid-sentence. He turned pale white as the blood drained from his face

"Good grief," he said, in shock. "You're the biggest man …," again, he stopped in mid-sentence. "I've ever seen." His voice started to crack, as he trembled

Hercules just smiled, showing his bright white teeth, and single gold tooth in the middle of the top row of his mouth. He then quickly pulled both revolvers from the pockets of two of the rednecks.

Should I hold these for you officer?" Hercules asked.

Cardinal pulled out his revolver and pointed it at the three rednecks. "I would appreciate it," Cardinal said.

Hercules Maxwell put both weapons in his pockets of his overalls. "I'm right here with you," he said to Bobby and smiled.

Bobby smiled back, as he told the three to get on their knees. Two of them dropped to their knees, immediately. The third loudmouthed, stringy haired one, who had the switch blade, started to raise the arm, which held the knife.

In the overall scheme of things, that redneck could very well have been raising his arm to hand the knife to Officer Cardinal. He was still in a state of shock from seeing the massive black man in front of him. Hercules Maxwell, however, did not want to take any chances, so he immediately grabbed the loudmouth redneck's wrist and squeezed. Excruciating pain shot from the stringy haired redneck's wrist, which now had five broken bones, to the top of his shoulders. He dropped the knife and fell to his knees, screaming.

Everybody in the bar clapped and cheered for both Bobby and Hercules.

"Hercules!" said Bobby, relaxing some, as his tone became a lot friendlier. "Are you okay? You're not in jail, are you?"

"No sir, I'm alright; but I've got some important info for you," he said.

"What is it?" He asked. He left the recorder running, in case he forgot some of Hercules' details.

Hercules Maxwell loved Roberto Cardinal like his own brother. He had shown on numerous occasions that he would willingly give up his own life for Bobby. Bobby Cardinal had mutual feelings for Hercules. Hercules explained to Bobby that he had some friends who were in desperate need of money, so they made a deal with a vicious member of the Dixie Mafia, whose name was Herman Friday. His friends were Frank and Evelyn Perry. They flew to Biloxi, Mississippi; and stayed at Beau Rivage Resort for two days, courtesy of Herman Friday and a guy by the name of Kirby Nox, Jr.

Hercules Maxwell's last statement caused a cold sweat to form along Cardinal's side and chest. He was now totally awake; and a chill ran down his entire body.

"Did you say Kirby Nox, Jr.?" asked Cardinal.

"That's right," said Hercules. "Why? Does that name mean something to you.?"

"Yes, it does," answered Cardinal. "I'll explain it later. Tell me the rest of your information."

Maxwell went on to explain that Frank and Evelyn Perry were given $225,000.00 up front to deliver a large load of cocaine and amphetamines which would be hidden in an RV that they would deliver to Birmingham, Alabama. They would be given an additional $275,000.00 upon arrival to a particular address in Birmingham. They would have to call Kirby Nox, Jr. from a pre-established location, which is a service station, at the intersection of Highway 27 and Interstate 20 West.

"That station's been abandoned for over six months," said Cardinal.

"I know. So, whatcha want to do?" asked Maxwell.

"You say that you know these people really well?" asked Cardinal.

"Yes, Sir. I do," he answered.

"What if you told them that I'd be there, and I could help them?" asked Cardinal.

"I was hoping that you would say that," said Hercules. "That would work. It's now twenty minutes till two. I'll call them and tell them to be there at the payphone at 2:30am. Would that give you enough time?"

"That would be plenty of time," said Bobby. "I'm less than fifteen minutes from the location, and there's obviously no traffic. I'll throw on some clothes; and start."

"Please don't leave, yet, Mr. Bobby," said Hercules. "I'm coming right over to your house; and I'm going with you. You might need a little extra protection."

Bobby Cardinal laughed. "I'll be okay, Hercules," he said. "You don't have to do that; although I really would love to have you with me. I haven't seen you in a while."

"I'll be right over, Major Cardinal," said Hercules. "I've always wanted to say that to you. Praise the Lord, I love you, Bobby!"

"And I love you, my brother in Christ," said Bobby, with a tear in his eye. "I'll see you in a couple of minutes."

Bobby Cardinal then pushed the stop button on the telephone recorder. He then got dressed. He strapped on his shoulder holster and inserted his Browning fourteen shot clip. He cranked one into the chamber and added one to the clip.

"Now it's a fifteen shot," he quietly said, as he grabbed two additional clips; and put on a light jacket to conceal his weapon.

He decided not to tell Jenny that he was leaving.

"There's no need to wake her; and cause her to worry, needlessly," he said quietly to himself. "Especially now, with the baby so close. She'll be mad; but I'll explain it in the morning. Besides this won't take that long. I'll probably be back, before she wakes up." He then nodded, as he justified his actions to his own satisfaction.

He then heard a car pull up to the curb, in front of his house. He quickly Stuck his mini tape recorder in the right pocket of his jacket. He then quickly ran to the front door and opened it just as Hercules was getting ready to push the doorbell.

"No," said Bobby, shaking his head. "You'll wake her."

"Oh, brother, I almost forgot," said Hercules. "Has she had the baby, yet?"

Bobby shook his head. He then embraced Hercules. "Thanks for doing this with me, man," he said.

"Thank you, for letting me!"

They then jumped into Bobby's Taskforce car and headed towards the payphone at the abandoned service station at the intersection of Interstate 20 and State Highway 27. They arrived at 2:31 am. At

2:37 am the Perrys showed up in the RV. Hercules had explained everything to them. They were delighted that Bobby Cardinal was going to help them. Evelyn Perry Opened her purse and pulled out the paper with the telephone number on it. She handed her purse to her husband and handed the paper, with the telephone number of Kirby Nox, Jr., to Bobby Cardinal. He held up the paper for her to dial. At exactly 2:47am she dropped numerous quarters into the pay slot, when she was told to do so by the operator.

"Hello," Nox answered, at exactly 2:48 am.

Roberto Cardinal turned in the direction of the RV, when he heard a repeated buzzing sound. In all probability, even if Roberto Cardinal, had recognized the sound as that of a detonator to the explosives which were packed in the RV, he could not have done anything different than what he did at that point in time. The RV EXPLODED!!!

The explosion was so horrific that it leveled the entire abandoned service station; and it even shook and scorched one of the pillars which supported that section of Interstate 20. In that instant, Bobby grasped the paper with Nox's telephone number and closed it into his fist. He then stuck his fist into his jacket, as if he were reaching for his weapon.

At 2:57am an old red Cadillac convertible, pulled into the rubble of the service station. The driver of the car put it in park and stepped out. He grabbed the pay phone which was dangling on its cord.

"Hey!" said a voice. "Are you still there?"

"Yeah, I'm still here," said Nox. "Who is this?"

"It's me, Herman; Herman Friday," he said. "There's so much smoke and explosive around here that it's affected my voice."

"You're right," said Nox. "Your voice sounded different and I couldn't tell. Well, it sounded like it went as planned. Is that right?"

"Yes sir!" said Friday. "Just as we planned!"

"The cop and that couple?" asked Nox.

"They're all dead," said Friday. "There's even a big black guy here. He must have been Cardinal's snitch."

"Great job, Herman," said Nox. "Get all of their Id's and let me talk to Vernon."

"He's not here, Boss," he answered. "He's still at my place."

"You still have that dump on Grant Avenue?" asked Nox. "Don't I pay you enough money to get a nice place?"

"Well, I could use a raise," said Herman.

"Don't push it," said Kirby Nox. "Tell Kimbrel to get back here. I need him in Biloxi for another job. Tell him the Mayor is giving us a problem. Now get those Id's and get going."

"I'll do it," said Friday; "but I can't get the Id's. There's a ton of sirens coming this way and they're close."

"I understand," said Nox. "Get out of there!"

Herman Friday immediately jumped into Vernon Kimbrel's Cadillac convertible and headed towards Interstate 20 East. As he got on the Interstate traveling East, he could see, what appeared to be an endless stream of red and blue lights, and a virtual cacophony of different sirens. They were all headed to the abandoned service station at the intersection of State Highway 27 and the overpass of Interstate 20. They were responding to a reported explosion.

Although it was a convertible; Herman Friday brazenly laughed out loud.

EIGHTEEN

THERE ARE NO WRITTEN, PUBLISHED, OR SPOKEN WORDS WHICH CAN possibly depict the pain and anguish which the Cardinal family felt, when they heard the news of Roberto's death. It would be virtually impossible to describe the emotions that James Banner went through, due to the loss of his Vietnam commanding officer and fellow Taskforce member. There were many times that the Metropolitan Atlanta Narcotics and Intelligence Task Force would come together and to establish a plan of action for extremely important cases. There were even times when they have a prayer before their meeting, to seek Our Lord's guidance.

The sheer magnitude of this case, however, caused James Banner to ask all sixty-one of his agents and staff to take part in a day long activity of prayer and seeking the guidance of God, and His Son, Our Lord Jesus Christ, in the achieving of justice for Hercules Maxwell, Evelyn and Frank Perry, and, of course, Roberto Cardinal. The day of Prayer was approved by Superintendent Bobby Moore, Chief Herbert Jenkins, and the attorney General of the State of Georgia, Arthur K. Bolton. Governor George Busbee would later issue a Proclamation declaring July 19th as Roberto Cardinal's Day in the State of Georgia.

The funeral for Bobby Cardinal was one of the most attended in the history of slain law enforcement officers in the State of Georgia. Some news commentators even stated that they thought it was the most attended in the country. It was estimated that more than 8,000 attendees were at the funeral. Police honor guards from 42 different agencies participated in the activity. The Cardinal Family agreed to hold the funeral service at the First Baptist Church of Carrollton, Georgia; because of the expected number who would be attending. No one, however, anticipated the 8,000 plus who did attend.

Both Major Jack Caldwell and Major James Banner decided to wait until after the funeral and the day of prayer to officially begin the investigation. United States Attorney General Benjamin Richard Civiletti assigned seven Federal agents to the Metropolitan Atlanta Narcotics and Intelligence Task Force to assist in the Cardinal investigation. He assigned two agents from the FBI, two from the DEA, two from the ATF, and one FBI profiler. The profiler was a well-known psychologist who had previously worked with the Veterans Administration. Her name was Dr. Amy Griner.

Amy had been recruited to the FBI by Tony "Rocky" Watson, the Special Agent in Charge (SAC) of the Atlanta Field Office. Tony was a Vietnam veteran, who suffered from Post-Traumatic Stress Disorder (PTSD). He met Amy Griner on several secret visits to the VA Medical Center in Decatur, Georgia—secret because he did not want the Bureau to know of his condition. Amy agreed to meet him outside of normal channels. After fourteen months of intensive treatments, both she and her supervisor, Dr. Isabella Amshire, agreed that Tony Watson could basically be declared as cured from PTSD.

"I don't think that anyone is completely cured from PTSD," Amy said to Tony. "If you had another traumatic situation in your life, it would obviously return. Working for the FBI makes that a very likely situation."

"Does that mean I will not ever be able to see you, again?" Tony asked Amy.

"Of course not!" She said emphatically. "You can see me anytime you want." She blushed and looked away from the young and handsome FBI agent.

Amy Griner was, as many would describe, 'drop dead gorgeous' to Tony Watson. Her desire to help him; and her ability to do so, made her even more attractive.

"Then how about if I have your private number, in the event I have an after-hours crisis?" Tony asked.

"I'll check with my supervisor and let you know," Amy responded, with a smile.

Tony leaned in, hugged her. They both noticed how nice it felt. Tony Watson then returned to work.

"I agreed to protect Agent Watson's career, by allowing you to keep his treatment off the record," Dr. Amshire said to Dr. Amy Griner. "I still believe, and I always will believe that we did the right thing. He is a good man, who has worked harder than any of our other patients to heal his disorder; and he seems to have succeeded. We owe him continued secrecy." She then put her hand on Amy's arm. "He is not officially your patient, Amy. As far as the VA is concerned you have never treated him, nor do you know him. After fourteen months, I think you know how you feel about him. What you do with those feelings is truly up to you and him."

Dr. Isabella Amshire touched the side of Amy's face and looked intently into her eyes. She then smiled and said, "God has someone special for you, Amy. Don't throw him away because of some misguided regulation."

Amy smiled and hugged Isabella.

"I don't know how to thank you," Amy said.

"Just follow your heart, Amy," Isabella replied.

The next day Dr. Amy Griner called Special Agent in Charge Tony Watson at his office. When he answered, she rattled off a series of numbers.

"What's that?" asked Tony.

"My private telephone number," she whispered.

"I'm sorry. Did you want to speak to Tony?" he said, in a slightly changed voice.

"I'm sorry." Amy blurted out in a very flustered voice. "I ... I thought that this was Agent Watson ... I mean in charge agent ... or whatever your or his ..."

"Amy, please slow down and please calm down. I was just kidding with you!" Tony said, while biting his lip to keep from laughing out loud.

"I can't believe you did that?" Amy's emotions were somewhere between the edge of laughter and the edge of tears. "I imagine that this line is recorded, so you probably already have my private number. Otherwise, I would change my mind and not give it to you," she quipped.

"Well, you do have to give it to me," said Tony; "because this is the only non-recorded line in the whole office. I had it put in because of my conversations with you, which I did want to keep secret. Remember?"

"Well after you pulled that little trick on me," she said with a hint of laughter in her voice, "Why should I give it to you, now?"

"Because, I'm in love with you Dr. Griner!" Tony Watson answered.

Amy's phone stayed silent for almost a full thirty seconds.

"I don't know what to say," Amy finally answered.

"You're an extremely intelligent and unbelievably beautiful young lady," said Tony; "who has dissected my mind, emotions, and very soul for over fourteen months. You know more about me, Amy Griner, than any other human being on the face of this earth; so, I knew that you knew how I felt about you. I'm totally in love with you, Amy, and that should not be a surprise to you, so what is your telephone number?"

"Please write it down this time," she said with the sweetest laugh in her voice. She then gave him her private number. "By the way, Tony, I need to tell you something."

"What is it, Amy?" He answered.

"I love you, too," she said softly; "and I want to become an FBI agent. We'll talk about it tonight, after you call me, and we have our first date."

She then smiled to herself and hung up. "I'm sure he knows, by now, that I will always have the last word."

After she hung up, Agent Watson quickly researched the FBI's Fraternalization Policy. He was then relieved, when he saw how vague and lax it was.

Dr. Amy Griner got her wish. She became an official FBI agent and went on to become a profiler. She was also instrumental in helping hundreds of Federal employees who were suffering from PTSD. She was working in the Atlanta Office, when the Roberto Cardinal murder occurred; and she requested to be assigned to the task force to assist. The SAC Tony Rocky Watson also recommended her. She got the assignment.

Major James Banner began the briefing. Major Jack Caldwell sat at a desk which was to Banner's left side. Banner went over the evidence found at the scene; including the recorder in Cardinal's jacket pocket; as well as the phone number which was clutched in his hand.

"It was a miracle that both the recorder and paper with the phone number for the hotel room in Biloxi, Mississippi, survived the explosion completely intact." Banner told the Taskforce members. "We also have Bobby's home telephone recorder. After listening to his last ... his last ... I'm so sorry ..." tears were freely flowing from Major Banner's eyes.

"What Jim is trying to say," interrupted Caldwell, as he put his hand on Banner's shoulder, and gently directed him to the chair on his right; "is that Bobby's home recorder gave us plenty of information about the setup and the people involved. His personal recorder in his jacket, however, identified the killers and the conspiracy which had taken place. We've traced the location of the call that the Perry's made to the Beau Rivage Resort Casino to a room that was occupied by Kirby McCord Nox, Jr. He is the reputed head of the Dixie Mafia."

"Was he the one that set off the bomb in the RV, remotely?" Amy Griner asked.

"That's an excellent point, Dr. Griner," Jack said, as he prepared to introduce her. "To those of you who don't know Dr. Amy Griner," he said, motioning for her to stand, which she did both blushing and with reluctance; "This is the renowned criminal profiler, Dr. Amy Griner."

Every taskforce member, federal agent, and staff member stood to their feet and gave her a standing ovation. Dr. Amy Griner had impacted most of the people in that room as either patients or their loved ones.

Once everyone had settled down; and Amy Griner was still red. Jack continued. "We don't have any solid evidence at this point to tell us how the bomb was detonated. The ATF is still working on several theories. The number one theory, however, is the belief that it was detonated remotely by a device which utilized a beeper and another telephone. We suspect that Herman Friday and Vernon Kimbrel, both notorious assassins for organized crime, were involved in planning, setting up, and implementing the bombing itself. Our strongest evidence, at this time, is against Herman Friday and Kirby Nox. We have them on Roberto Cardinal's recorder, which was in his jacket, admitting to the bombing and the killing of the four victims."

"Then what are we waiting for?" one of the agents yelled out. "Let's get out there and nail those thugs."

Jack Caldwell calmly looked down for a second. He then raised his head and spoke with both determination and fortitude. "I can promise you that we will very professionally, and with the highest level of accuracy and diligence, investigate this case; and then we will absolutely NAIL THOSE WOTHLESS PIECES OF WASTE TO THE DEATH PENALTY!"

Once again, the room erupted with applause.

Major James Banner, the minister, looked directly at Major Jack Caldwell, the cop, and smiled. He then stood up and applauded as tears continued to flow down his cheeks. Jack rushed to his partner and embraced him.

"Go ahead, my dear friend," Jack said, as he held Banner's head in the hollow of his shoulder. "Now it's your time to grieve. Just let it out. I've got you. Just let it out."

NINETEEN

THAT NIGHT, AS JAMES BANNER HELD HIS WIFE CLOSE TO HIM, IN bed; he could feel her heart beating against his chest. He loved that feeling. There were times when he couldn't tell which heart was beating, his or hers. He slowly and gently pulled her a little closer to him, until he could feel her rhythmic breathing against the top of his shoulder.

"I love you, so much," he whispered.

"I love you, too," she responded, as she had done so many times in the past.

James knew that her response was probably automatic; and she was still asleep. It touched him deeply to realize that her body and mind were off somewhere in dreamland; but her soul was still connected to his. Feeling very anxious and worried about the interview with Herman Friday in the morning, he decided to pray. He asked for wisdom and guidance; but he mainly asked that God's will be done; and God's Glory be manifested.

Surprisingly, he almost immediately fell asleep. His sleep was deep and extremely restful. He knew he was dreaming; but it seemed too real to be a dream. He dreamt about Roberto Cardinal; and a conversation, which they were having. Roberto was advising him on what to do and say in the interview with Friday. He also dreamt that someone else was with Roberto. The person behind Roberto was so bright that he could barely see him. He appeared to be a figure that was brighter than a golden sun. There also appeared to be a crown on His head.

Suddenly Cardinal disappeared and only the sun-like figure remained. His voice seemed to encompass every sense and emotion that Banner felt. It also filled James Banner with calm and peace.

"Remember Herman Friday's son," the voice said. "Fear not. This is my battle I will be fighting it for you."

Banner abruptly awoke. Then the alarm went off. Barbara Banner pushed the off button and arose.

"Jim? Time to get up," she said.

When she turned to look at him, she was surprised to see that he was already sitting on the edge of the bed.

"I guess you really are anxious to interview that killer today," she said. "Did you get any sleep?"

"I don't think I've ever slept that deep in my life," he answered. "I had the sweetest and the scariest dream."

"Do you want to or have time to tell me about it?" she asked.

"Let me take a shower and get dressed; then I will."

James Banner told his wife every detail. She hung on every word. She then took his hand; and pulled him towards her. She then gently kissed him.

"I believe you, Jim. I also believe that God spoke to you through Roberto and His Son, Jesus."

"What am I supposed to do?" he asked.

Barbara looked at her husband, and her sparkling hazel eyes seemed to know exactly what to say. It was, as if, God had His Lips pressed against her ear.

"Do exactly what Our Lord told you to do." Barbara said very tenderly. "Just follow His guidance, which He'll place in your heart. Don't forget, this is His fight." She then gently touched the right side of his cheek. "Remember Jim, just like the situation that happened, years ago, with that nurse."

A light seemed to sparkle in Banner's eyes. "That's right. Her name was Jillian Anders," Banner remembered.

"Just like that same incident, my darling," Barbara continued. "Just be patient and wait for Him to win it for you."

Banner smiled and cupped his wife's face in his hands.

"Next to Our Lord, Jesus Christ," he said; "you and our kids are the best gifts that God has ever lent me."

Barbara Banner stood and pulled her husband close to her. Their lips met, and she let herself peacefully melt into his embrace. He gently pulled her even closer, and then lifted her off of her feet.

"I love you, so very much," he said as tears began to well up in his eyes

"I love you even more," she said resting her head in the hollow of his shoulder. "You complete me. Jim; we are one." She then slowly tapped his shoulder, as he lowered her.

"Speaking of kids," she said. "You've never missed one of Scott's games; so, don't worry about today." She smiled, "I've already taken care of it. I told him that today is a very important day for you and you might not be able to make the game. He took it very well; and he completely understood,"

"I'm sure he understood, as well as, any six-year-old could understand," Banner replied. "I'm sure that Kelly will cheer enough for all of us. She may only be two, but she has a great set of lungs."

"She's going to soon be three," Barbara interjected; "as she often reminds us."

"Thank you, Honey. I really don't deserve you."

Barbara immediately put her hand to Jim's mouth. "I told you, many times before, do not ever say that." A smile crossed her lips. "Tiffany's dad, Rev. Emory Green, has told us that he was absolutely sure that God put us together for a reason. When you say, you don't deserve me, you're doubting God's wisdom". Her voice then became very firm. "You do deserve me; and I deserve you! God does not make mistakes!"

James Banner smiled and wrapped his arms around her. He didn't want her to see the tear that was falling from his eye.

"Thank you," he said, still holding her. "You always know exactly what to say."

Maj. James Banner hummed as he drove to the Task Force office. He pulled into the parking space marked with his name. It was the first one in the row which was marked 'Staff Parking Only'. Next to his was the one marked 'Commander Jack Caldwell'. It pleased him that after all these years, they were still side by side. The next spot, however, was for Dr. Amy Griner. Caldwell insisted that she have the spot next to him.

As Banner stepped out of a brand new 1982 maroon Chevrolet Impala, he noticed the Federal prison van parked against the curb outside of the entrance to the Metropolitan Atlanta Narcotics and Intelligence Task Force Office. Two massive Federal Prison guards were leading Herman Friday, whose arms and legs were shackled; and a heavy chain was utilized to connect his extremities to each other. In fact, he was restrained to the point that he barely could walk. Friday was a slender man, thirty-two years old, who was six feet, two inches tall, and weighed 187 lbs. He had dark black hair and cold brown eyes. There was a deep, jagged scar on his forehead from a broken beer bottle, which he had gotten in a bar-fight with a drunken opponent. The opponent had a much worse scar across his throat, which left him dead. Herman Friday claimed self-defense and the jury believed him.

Herman Friday's skin was heavily scared from acne. He also walked with a slight limp on his left leg, from a broken knee cap, which he received from the police. His attempt to run from the police, when he was a teenager, was met by a night stick to his left knee.

Friday was held on each side by the guards, who literally were lifting him and carrying him to the front door. As they were about to press the buzzer on the entrance panel, Banner interrupted them.

"Hold on, officers," Banner said. "I'll let you in. I'm not sure if anyone is up there this early. I'm usually the first one here."

He then pulled out his key and manually unlocked the front metal door. Jack Caldwell then pulled up and several other agents and staff also began to caravan into the staff parking area. Dr. Amy Griner was among them, pulling up in a 1981 Mercedes Benz. Jack Caldwell watched as she parked in her assigned space, next to his. He then opened her door. Everyone knew that Major Caldwell deliberately selected that space for her; for the sole purpose of watching her get out of and get into her car. She stepped out of her vehicle wearing her mini skirt, unaware of all that she was revealing, she gave Jack a very sweet smile. He returned the smile, as a drop of sweat formed on his forehead.

By the time they had all arrived upstairs, the building seemed to turn into organized chaos.

"Put him in the interrogation room," Jack, standing outside his office, said to the guards.

"Take off all of his shackles, except for his handcuffs," said James Banner, who was standing next to Jack. "Make sure the handcuffs are run through the iron ring on his side of the interrogation table."

Both guards nodded, in acknowledgement.

"Jack, I need to talk to you, in private," said Banner; "before we go in there. Amy too."

"Sure," Jack answered, "I'll get her. We can meet in your office in a couple of minutes."

Banner nodded.

"Anything wrong?" Amy asked, as she and Caldwell entered into Major Banner's office.

"No," said Banner. "I just need to run something by you guys." He then explained his dream to both of them. He even told them the part about 'Remembering Herman Friday's son.'

"Dreams are generally thoughts that are hidden deep in our subconscious," Amy said. "Many psychologists believe that they are the result of our anxieties. It's the way that the brain uses to connect our subconscious with reality. Christians believe that it is a way that God uses to talk to His believers."

"So, you think that God was actually speaking to me?" Banner asked.

"I don't know, Jim," she answered. "Most Christians, generally I mean, believe that He does it through His Word, the Bible. If you don't read the Bible that much, then I suppose you could honestly believe that He spoke to you in a vision."

"What's the difference between a vision and a dream?" asked Caldwell.

"A dream is seldom remembered. At best, if you were to wake up and immediately try to write down your dream; you would probably remember less than 5% of what you had been dreaming. A vision is more like what Jim is describing," Amy continued. "He remembers unique details like the bright light, especially the crown on His head; and how He spoke to him. He also remembers every detail that Roberto told him. The only conclusion for such details is either James Banner is lying, or he had a true vision."

Both Banner and Caldwell looked shocked.

Dr. Amy Griner smiled and said, "I know he's not lying, so quit acting so surprised."

"Thank you, both," Banner said, as he stood up. "I think I'm ready to begin with Friday's interview."

"I'll get together all of the information on his son, which I've already been researching; in order to get a better understanding of Mr. Friday," said Amy. "By the way, his son's name is Clark. He just turned seven about two months ago; and Friday loves him more than anything else on the face of this earth."

"Thank you, Amy," said Banner. "Bring the information to me in the interview room, when you get it."

Dr. Amy Griner nodded and left.

Both Jack Caldwell and James Banner took a moment to pray for wisdom and guidance, before they entered the interrogation room

"Well it's about time," yelled Herman Friday, as Banner and Caldwell stepped into the interview room.

"What's the matter, scumbag," Jack Caldwell said sarcastically; "do you have some special date or event that you have to attend?"

"You're one piece of dog crap," Friday shouted at Caldwell. "Let me tell you right now, I ain't saying nothing to you two. You can jabber all you want; and you can even beat me, until I'm half dead. I've been through a lot worse than what you two can think of; and I ain't never talked. I don't intend to do none now, and I'm not a 'scumbag'."

Herman Friday then slammed both hands on the metal table, which was bolted to the floor.

"For a guy who is not talking, you sure do a lot of explaining, and you certainly are not a 'scum bag' Mr. Friday." Banner said.

Herman Friday seemed to freeze in his tracks. His growling face took on a calmer demeanor. "That's funny," he softly said. "You must be the one they call the minister. Is, that, right?"

"That's right, Mr. Friday," said Banner, softly and firmly. "I just need to ask you some simple questions; then I'll try to get you out of here, as soon as I can. I know you're busy; and I don't want to take up too much of your time."

"Now, that's respect!" Friday said, as he looked directly at Caldwell. "this man here knows how to show respect. I don't mind talking to gentlemen, who are respectful."

"Yeah, right!" said Caldwell as he sat down next to Banner and across from Friday. He then noticed that Banner had finished writing something on the notepad, which was hidden in the file he was holding up.'

The paper on the notepad, which was away from Friday's line of sight simply said:

"I'M FOLLOWING THE SCRIPT THAT ROBERTO CARDINAL TOLD ME LAST NIGHT!"

Jack Caldwell made a very slight inconspicuous nod.

At that time, Amy Griner knocked on the door.

"I'm sorry for the interruption, Mr. Friday," said Banner, politely. "Just give me a second to answer this." He got up to let Amy come in.

Friday looked directly at Caldwell another time. He gnarled his face, showing complete and total contempt. He then pointed to Banner, who was opening the door. He spit out the word "RESPECT."

Caldwell just rolled his eyes.

"I have that file you wanted, Mr. Banner," said Amy.

"Thank you, so much, Dr. Griner," James said, as he took the file from her hand.

Amy turned and started to leave, when Banner touched her

shoulder. "Wait a minute, Amy." He said. "I truly did not mean to be so rude," Banner said to Friday. "Herman, may I call you Herman?"

"Of course," Friday nodded.

I want to introduce you to Dr. Amy Griner. She works with us here at the Task Force."

"It's a pleasure to meet you," said Amy, who realized what James was doing. She then extended her hand.

Herman Friday attempted to reach her hand; but was restrained by the locked-down chain on his handcuffs. Amy, politely, leaned over enough to reach his hand and shake it.

"Thank you," said Friday. "That was very nice of you." He, once again, looked at Caldwell.

"I know," interrupted Caldwell. "Respect!!! You don't have to say it. I get it."

You could probably count on one hand the number of times that Herman Friday had smiled in his lifetime; and this was one of those times.

"Do you mind if Dr. Griner sits in here and takes notes?" Banner asked Friday.

"I would be honored to have such a great looking broad to look at," Friday answered, as he smiled at Amy.

"Thank you, Mr. Friday," she said. "I'm very flattered."

"If this continues, I might just puke," Caldwell said, very softly.

Major James Banner then moved in for the kill. He got up and walked around the table and stood by Herman Friday's side. He then put a sheet of paper down in front of Friday and leaned over to explain it.

"I got it," said Herman Friday, as he took the pen from Major James Banner's hand and signed his 'Waiver of Right's' form. "I know my rights," he calmly said, "and I'm waiving them. You and Miss Amy and even Mr. disrespectful, over there, can ask me whatever you want."

Banner, Caldwell, and Griner were speechless for a few seconds. This was definitely not what they expected.

"Thank You, Our Lord," Banner mumbled under his breath. "This battle is Yours."

James Banner returned to his seat directly across from Friday. He then began by asking him some basic preliminary questions about where he was born, how long was he in Georgia, and what type of work he did. The questioning went on for about ten minutes, when Herman Friday stood up and struck the table with the palms of his hands.

"Please excuse me for saying this, Miss Amy," he said to Dr. Amy Griner. "Why don't we skip all of this bull and you ask me about my killing those four people, including that cop!"

Once again, all three went into a semi-shock.

"Okay," said Banner. "That's a good point. We can cut the preliminaries. Why don't you tell us about how you went about murdering Mr. and Mrs. Perry, Hercules Maxwell, and Captain Roberto Cardinal, on that early Sunday morning of April 19, 1981, at the intersection of Highway 27 and the Interstate 20 overpass, at 2:48 am, by causing an RV to explode. The same RV which you rigged with C4 explosives and a detonator."

"Everything you said is totally right," said Friday, "except for one thing. I didn't pack or rig those explosives. My job was to simply to detonate them."

"Then who ..." Jack Caldwell started to ask, but Banner's touch on the back of his shoulder stopped him

"Just tell us, in your own words, what happened from beginning to end," said James Banner. "You do realize, Mr. Friday, that this entire conversation has been and continues to be recorded."

"I sure do, and I completely approve," said Friday.

Both James Banner and Jack Caldwell were totally at a loss. When they looked at Amy, she just shrugged her shoulders, masking disbelief. Friday gave them every detail of the plan to execute both Roberto Cardinal and Hercules Maxwell. He called the Pettys "collateral damage." The one primary thing he did not talk about were the names and involvement of any other individuals.

"You do realize that you could receive the death penalty for what you have just admitted to doing," Caldwell said. "I am saying that with the deepest respect for you Mr. Friday."

"Thank you, for saying that Major Caldwell. I am aware of what my penalty might be; and I'm ready to pay for my sins."

"What Jack is also trying to say," interjected James Banner, "is the fact that you don't have to get the death penalty; if you tell us who else was involved in the conspiracy to do this. We know you're an enforcer for the Dixie Mafia," Banner continued. "That would indicate that someone hired you to do this. If that's the case, then tell us who it was, and we'll be able to make a deal with you, that could save your life."

"I really do know what you're saying," said Herman Friday, "but there's no way that I can tell you anyone else's name."

Lowering his head, Friday looked down at his handcuffed arms. It seemed to the others he was signaling the finality of his statement. They were wrong.

"You are right, Major Banner," Friday said. "I was hired and helped by others to do this; but, as I said earlier, there is absolutely no way in hell that I'll rat them out."

Banner, looking directly into Friday's eyes, saw concern and fear in his gaze. Banner glanced over at Dr. Griner; and she instinctively understood.

"You need to think about your son, Herman," Amy said. "I know that Clark is a very important part of your life. If someone has threatened to harm him, we can stop them; and keep him safe."

Herman Friday jerked upright, staring straight at her. His eyes were now filled with terror; tears were beginning to flow. His gaze, however, shifted to the left of Amy Griner, to a blank wall behind her. His eyes seemed to slightly enlarge with more fear and horror.

"I'm begging you. Please, don't hurt him. He's only five years old." Friday spoke in a highly-stressed voice; and one that was terrified.

Amy motioned for both Caldwell and Banner to leave the room; which they immediately did. They watched through the two-way mirror the incident that was unfolding in the interrogation room. Dr. Griner was attempting to calm down Herman Friday. When she touched his hand, he seemed to return to reality. Tears were streaking down his face.

"Is ... Is ... Is the minister still here?" Friday's question was in the form of a plea. "I'm begging you doctor, please. I need to talk to the minister."

Amy nodded at the two-way mirror; and James Banner walked in and looked directly at Herman Friday.

"Why did you need to see me?" Banner asked Friday.

The cold-blooded killer, who was now in tears, looked up at Banner and clenched his fists.

"You have got to save him!" Friday said vehemently. "I'm begging you. I'll tell you everything you want to know about that murder; and I'll tell you everyone who is involved. I'll even testify against them; if you ..." Herman Friday began to choke on his own sobs. He grabbed the bottle of water next to him; Amy opened it for him.

"Drink slowly," she said. "That's good. Now take slow deep breaths." Friday slowly began to regain his composer.

"Is it your son that you want me to save?" asked Banner.

Herman Friday vigorously nodded his head. "Please! Please! You're the only one who can save him. I swear on my son's soul that I'll tell you everything. Just save my boy."

"I need to know what kind of danger he's in, who has him, and if you have any idea as to where he is right now?"

Once again, Friday vigorously nodded his head. "He's in danger of giving his soul to Satan. He's at my home in Villa Rica, with a baby sitter. He's also at the brink of the abyss."

"How do you know this?" asked Jack Caldwell, who had entered the room a few minutes earlier.

"BECAUSE I SAW HIM," Friday shouted out. "He was right here. He was being held by the devil. Satan, himself, the filthy liar, was holding my baby boy in his arms. He was laughing. Both Vernon and Kirby were right behind Satan; and THEY WERE ALSO LAUGHING."

Dr. Griner placed her hand on Herman's left shoulder. He looked up at her; and gently placed his head against her caring hand. He then let his tears roll down his face and onto her fingers. She then softly placed her other hand on the right side of his face.

"Just cry all you need to," she said. "We're here; and we will save your son, Clark. I promise you, Herman, that we will do it; and we'll do it today."

"Thank you!" He said to Amy. He then twisted his head and kissed her hand, which was still on his left shoulder.

TWENTY

"I THINK I KNOW WHAT HE WANTS ME TO DO," SAID JAMES BANNER; "But I need to go alone."

"There is absolutely no way on the face of this earth, that you're going alone." Jack Caldwell said.

"Okay," said Banner; "but you'll have to wait in the car while I go inside his house, alone."

Jack nodded in agreement.

"Then I'm coming with the two of you." Amy Griner insisted. "I have no problem with waiting in the car."

"Okay," Banner said. "Let's mount up!"

The drive to Herman Friday's home in Villa Rica was exactly 43 minutes. When they arrived at the corner of Cleghorne Drive and Russell Street, they pulled into Friday's driveway. The door to the one-story ranch house was partially open and a small child was standing in the doorway.

As Banner exited the vehicle, he reminded both Caldwell and Dr. Griner that they would wait in the car. He then walked to the front door and held out his hand to the seven-year old. They looked nothing alike, but he could not help but think of his own son, Scott. A young, slim, red haired woman appeared in the front entrance. She motioned for him to come in.

"My name is James Banner," he said looking at the seven-year old.

"I know who you are," Clark said, as he shook his hand. "That man who just left told us you were coming."

"What man?" Banner asked in as calm a voice as he could muster while looking towards the young lady.

"My name is Brittany," she said, extending her hand.

"I'm from the Metropolitan Atlanta Narcotics and Intelligence Task Force," said Banner. "Who was the man, he's talking about?" he repeated.

"He said his name was Roberto Cardinal," she answered. "He also told us about you, and you would be coming to save Clark."

James Banner stopped dead in his tracks, his hand still as he held on to Brittany's hand. "What did you say his name was?" His voice cracked, and his heart began to beat rapidly.

"I'll tell you everything," Brittany smiled; "if you release my hand and come in."

"I'm so sorry," Banner said with an awkward smile, following her into the living room.

"It was as if he came out of nowhere," she began. "Either that or he came directly from heaven," she smiled.

"She's smiling as if she knows a lot more than what she's saying," Banner thought. He also knew, as he looked deeply into her shimmering hazel eyes, that this young lady was not able to lie. She was speaking with the purest of innocence.

"You're just like Barbara," he mistakenly said out loud.

"Is Barbara your wife?" Brittany asked. Her question almost seemed rhetorical.

"Yes," Banner answered, with a red face. "I'm so sorry. That just seemed to blurt out."

"That's fine," she said, still smiling. "That's exactly what happened, sir; and now you're here, just as Roberto said."

"Thank you, Brittany. I completely believe you and I do understand. Do you know what Roberto meant by my saving Clark?" Banner asked.

"Yes," answered Brittany. "Roberto said that you would lead Clark to Our Lord, Jesus Christ; and Jesus would come into his heart and save him. His soul would be sealed for heaven for all eternity." Her eyes looked like bright stars in a green sea. "Isn't that right?"

James Banner nodded. He then touched the side of her cheek, amazed. He took in a deep breath and rested his eyes on the child.

"This is what Mr. Cardinal told you?" Banner asked Clark.

"You mean Major Cardinal, don't you?" Clark asked.

Major James Banner could barely keep the tears from falling.

"What's wrong?" Clark asked. "Did I say something bad?" His face changed to worry. "Please sir don't cry. I'm sorry ... I'm so sorry."

"Oh no," said Banner, smiling through his tears. "Everything you said is so joyful, and so beautiful and so right. You have done absolutely nothing wrong."

"Then why are you crying?" His innocence overwhelmed this co-commander.

"Sometimes, we adults cry when we are so happy," said Banner. "I know it sounds crazy, but that's the way God made us."

Seven-year-old Clark Friday pretended to understand.

"I'm going to bring some people in here," said Banner to both Brittany and Clark.

"I'll get them for you," Brittany volunteered and immediately ran towards the car in the driveway. She ran with such enthusiasm, she almost seemed to fly across the lawn. It was difficult for Banner to tell if her feet were touching the ground. He could hear her excitement as she spoke into the open window of the car.

"Come in!' Come in, please." Her voice seemed to sing as she spoke. "The Lord God Almighty is about to enter Clark's heart. Soon all heaven will be singing. All heavenly host are about to have a party. You can't miss it. Please come in."

Dr. Amy Griner looked at this precious young lady almost glowing with joy; and their hearts connected. She then opened the car door and immediately embraced her. The floodgates of their souls burst open. For no known reason, as James Banner said, they cried because they were so happy.

"What's going on?" asked Caldwell.

"Just follow us," Amy yelled to him as she held Brittany's hand and ran towards the house.

Once they entered the house, they could see the young

seven-year-old on his knees, his hands folded, and his eyes closed. The edges of his blond hair rested on his ears; and his bangs were over half-an-inch from his eyebrows. The dimples on his cheeks seemed to be blushing. His face was lit up with a beautiful smile.

"He looks just like an angel, sent directly from heaven," Amy softly said.

"I agree," said Jack, as he gently touched her arm.

Brittany stood there, with her eyes closed, and her arms raised with open palms, quietly singing, "Praise the Lord God, Almighty! Praise His Holy Name!" She continued to sing as James Banner spoke to Clark.

"Clark Friday," said James. "Do you believe in Our Lord, Jesus Christ?"

"YES, I DO," Clark yelled.

His enthusiastic response caused Banner to smile. "Do you believe that He is your Lord and Savior?" Jim asked. "You may answer softly."

"Oh yes," said the precious seven-year-old. "He has saved me from the fires of the abyss; and He has given me eternal life. I will live with God, in heaven, forever."

"How did He do that?" asked Banner

"He suffered and died on the cross, for my sins, and the sins of the world," said Clark. Then his brow furrowed. "Why would He do that? Why would He let them beat Him, and whip Him, and let them make fun of Him? If that wasn't bad enough, He also let them nail Him to a cross?" Tears began to form in his heavenly blue eyes. "Why wouldn't His Daddy stop them?"

James Banner knelt and pulled the child to his chest. Brittany and Amy knelt on the side of Clark. All their faces, including Caldwell's, were covered in tears. Banner wiped the tears from his eyes and swallowed hard. He did not want Clark to think he was sad or upset.

"It's because His Daddy," said Banner, very softly, "did not want you to be punished for your sins. He wanted His Son to take all of the pain and punishment away from you."

"Why?" Clark asked, with pure innocence.

"Because He loves you so much!" both Amy and Brittany said in unison.

"I want to tell my daddy about this," Clark said. "Can I please do that?"

"Of course," answered Banner, looking to Caldwell. "We'll see if we can get him on the phone."

Jack then went with Brittany to find the telephone. A few minutes later he had Herman Friday on the line of the interrogation room telephone.

"I want you to talk to someone who loves you very much," Caldwell said. He then motioned to Banner to bring Clark into the room.

"This is your daddy," he said to Clark, as he handed him the phone.

"Daddy?" Clark Friday asked.

"Oh, Clark," answered Herman, in almost absolute disbelief. "Is that you?"

"Yes, Daddy! It's me." His voice was filled with joy. "Daddy! I've been saved! Jesus is in my heart! I now belong to God! Isn't that wonderful, daddy?"

"Oh, my precious son. Yes, it is." Herman Friday held back the tears, as he began to choke up. "I'm so happy, for you. I wish I could see you, my son." He knew the tears were about to break loose. "Please let me talk to one of the men there."

"Okay, Daddy", Clark said, as he handed the phone to Banner. "He wants to talk to you."

"Herman, this is Jim Banner," he said.

"I can only say, thank you, Major Banner," Friday said as the tears flowed down his face. "You have no idea, as to how grateful I am. My boy means everything to me. I will never be able to repay you for this."

The man who was responsible for 47 cold-blooded killings was now crying like a baby. They were not tears of remorse, however; they were tears of joy for his son. It was the first time, in his entire life, that he felt compassion; and he had no idea how to deal with that emotion.

"It's not me you have to repay, Herman," Banner said very softly.

"Roberto Cardinal is the one who caused your son to be saved." Banner looked at Caldwell and motioned for him to take Clark into the next room.

"How can I do that?" Friday asked. "He's dead! I killed him! I can never undo that! As God is my judge, I wish I could—but I can't." His tears now turned to remorse.

When Banner was certain that Clark could not hear the conversation, he said, "You can't undo it; but you can give him, and the other people you blew up, justice. You can tell us everything that happened and who was involved, including the people who hired you!"

There was a long pause on the other end of the phone. After two minutes of pure silence, Banner asked, "Are you still there?"

"Yes," Friday answered, very slowly. "I'll do exactly as you ask, on one condition."

James Banner's face became flush with anger. What right does this cold-blooded animal have to set conditions. How dare him. I can't wait to tell him no.

"What is your condition?" he asked very calmly, but firmly.

"I don't want anything in return! I want what I deserve; and I know that's the death penalty." Friday's voice became very cold. "I'll even testify against them. Every one of them.". I know the jury will believe me, when they realize that I'm going to be executed." He paused for a minute while he wiped the tears from his eyes and swallowed. "I do want somebody to take care of my baby boy. I know you are a man of your word. That's why they call you the minister. Give me your word Major Banner that you'll see to it my son is properly taken care of. That's all I want; and I'll tell you everything."

James Banner could not believe his ears. He stood, holding the phone, and turned pale white. He finally spoke, "You have my word, Herman. As the Lord God Almighty is my Judge, I give you my word."

"Jim, what is it? What's wrong?" asked Amy Griner. "What did he want?"

Banner just shook his head and put out his hand to let her know that everything was okay.

"We'll talk more about it when I get back," Banner said to Friday. "In the meantime, do you want to talk to your son, again?"

"Oh, yes, I really do," said Friday, with a huge smile on his face. "Mr. Banner ... I mean Major Banner, you're not just a minister; you're a saint."

TWENTY-ONE

HERMAN FRIDAY SPENT THE NEXT THREE DAYS WRITING HIS statement. He used three legal pads and wrote nearly 287 pages in long hand. After he finished, three secretaries worked around the clock for the next thirty-six hours, transcribing his manuscript. It translated into 183 pages, which were typed and double spaced. James Banner insisted that Friday sign both handwritten and typed copies of his statement, which he gladly did. It was a virtual history and development of the Dixie Mafia. He described all 47 murders which he had committed for Kirby Nox; and how Vernon Kimbrel helped him with most of them, including the murder of Jimmy Counter and his wife.

"I can't get my mind off what happened at Friday's house," said Dr. Amy Griner. "It's been almost a week and I still dream about it every night."

"The same dream?" Jack asked.

"Exactly as it really did happen," she said. "I have a PhD in psychology, and I can't explain it."

"I have a Masters' in Criminal Justice," said Banner; "But I can explain it."

"Then explain it to us!" Both Amy and Jack said at the same time.

"Don't look for your answers in this world," said Banner. "Your answers are in God." He then quietly got up and started towards the door. "I have faith in the two of you. You'll figure it out." He then turned and looked directly at Jack Caldwell. "Remember the nurse." He then opened the door and walked out.

"What is he talking about?" asked Amy.

"It's something that happened years ago," answered Jack. "When we were just detectives."

"We don't have anything pressing;" said Amy; "so, tell me what happened."

"It's kinda crazy, are you sure you want to hear about it? It will only add to your confusion."

"Just tell me," said Amy, with a slightly irritated voice.

"Okay," quipped Jack. "Do you want me to go back to the beginning?"

"Jack Caldwell! You're starting to get on my nerves! Just tell the story."

"It was about 5:00 pm and both Jim and I happened to be at the North Precinct in Sandy Springs." Caldwell began. "It started to rain, and wrecks were happening all over the place. If the afternoon rush hour wasn't enough; the wrecks stressed the police manpower to the breaking point."

"I can only imagine," Amy stated. "I've been on Roswell Road during rush hour. It's literally like a parking lot!"

"So, you know what I'm talking about," continued Caldwell. "Captain Schackelford was the evening watch Captain. Both Jim and I really admired him a lot; and we still do. He was looking very frustrated and talking on the telephone to some psychiatrist. We overheard him telling the doctor that what he was requesting was almost impossible, because almost every car he had was out handling wrecks; and they had to prioritize each call."

"What did he want him to do?" asked Amy.

"I'm getting to that," answered Caldwell. "Don't get ahead of the story."

Amy Griner nodded in acknowledgement.

"We overheard Capt. Schackelford tell the Psychiatrist that it was just across the street, so he'd go himself," continued Caldwell. "He was that kind of leader. He would not ask his men to do anything he, himself, was not willing to do. James, trying to impress the captain, quickly jumped in; and told him that we weren't doing anything, now, and did he need our help?" Jack Caldwell laughed. "He was always doing stuff like that. He, not only, would blindly jump into various situations; but also, volunteer me to do it with him; without asking me."

A smile crossed Amy Griner's face.

"Captain Schackelford was very grateful and appreciative of the help, especially at a time like that," Jack said. "He told us that Dr. William Michaelson, was a Psychiatrist and a patient of his, by the name of Jillian Anders, lived at the Valley Apartments, directly across from the precinct, and he needed a 'welfare check' on her. She was a nurse at Northside Hospital and she had gotten a particular bad performance review from her supervisor that afternoon; and he needed to know if she was okay. He had been trying to reach her, over the phone, for the past forty-five minutes and she wasn't answering. He didn't think she'd harm herself; but he was worried, since, in the past, she would call him right back."

"Was she okay?" asked Amy.

"You sure are impatient," said Caldwell, with a smile. "You need to drink less caffeine."

Griner nodded.

"Anyway," continued Jack; "the Captain said that she lived in Building B Apartment number 187. I probably should have known better, but I went with James to her apartment. We went to the front door and rang the doorbell; but there was no answer. After a few more rings on the doorbell, Banner, who was as impatient as you," Caldwell said, looking directly at Amy, "opened the screen door and started to knock loudly. "Finally, we could hear a female voice, from the inside, telling us to 'wait a minute'. She then asked who it was. After we told her that we were the police; she asked if anything was wrong. James told her that Dr. Michaelson was worried about her; and he wanted us to make sure that she was okay. When she answered that she was fine, I said 'great' and started to leave. When I motioned for James to come with me, he gave me that look."

Dr. Amy Griner looked puzzled. "What kind of look?" she asked.

"It was the way he furrowed his brow, and squinted his right eye," answered Caldwell. "It was his way of saying that there was something wrong, here. I have to admit that he had a special talent that could sense when something wasn't right. All the years that I've known him, he seems to have had that gift." Jack Caldwell stopped for a minute and stared at the window, as if in deep thought.

"I'm sorry," said Caldwell; as he snapped back to reality. "I must be boring myself. I started to drift off."

"Do you often do that?" laughed Dr. Amy Griner.

Jack only smiled.

"James was right," he continued. "As soon as we started to leave, we heard her say that she needed our help. She wanted one of us to come around to the outside of her apartment to her bedroom window. She said she was unable to get to the front door; and she needed someone to help her. James, of course, immediately went to her aid; and he told me to wait at the front door, which I did."

Jack Caldwell then shook his head. "I should have known that this whole thing was crazy, when she asked just one of us to come to the outside of the apartment to her bedroom window. James, however, being the knight in shining armor, had to go galloping off on his white stallion to save the damsel in distress. Little did he know what was getting ready to happen. If he did, I hope to believe that he would have been more cautious."

"What did happen?" Amy asked.

"A cop's worst nightmare," Caldwell answered.

Dr. Amy Griner's eyes widened; and she moved her chair closer to Jack; intent on hearing every word.

Jack smiled, milking the suspense to the very limit.

"Come on, Jack," she insisted. "Finish the story. What happened, next?"

Jack leaned in a little closer to her. "She was pulling at the screen to her window; and she asked James to help her remove the screen, which he did. After he pulled the screen off, he laid it on the ground and when he stood up he was facing the barrel of a .38 caliber snub-nose revolver which was touching his forehead."

At that time Amy put her hand to her mouth and blurted out, "Did she kill him!"

Jack looked at her and couldn't help but laugh.

"He just walked out of here, Miss Phd in Psychology and he looked very much alive.".

Amy blushed and asked Jack to please continue.

"James asked her, what she was doing?' continued Caldwell. "She answered, in a very 'matter of fact' voice that she wanted to commit suicide. James has always used humor as a defense mechanism."

Amy nodded in acknowledgement.

"He said that she was pointing the gun in the wrong direction," Caldwell said, with a slight laugh. "She told him that he was funny, and she liked that; but she was serious. She went on to say that she did not have the nerve to kill herself; so, she figured, that if she shot him then the other officers would kill her."

"Suicide by cop," Amy replied.

Jack nodded. "When James pointed out that there were no other cops around, she nodded and told him to push the red button on his radio."

"The red button?" Amy Griner said looking very confused.

"It's this button here," Jack said, pointing to a small red button on the top of his radio. "It sends a signal to the communications room, alerting the radio operators that an officer is in trouble and needs help right away. It also acknowledges the fact that an officer is being held hostage."

Dr. Griner started to touch the button, but immediately pulled her hand back.

"Miss Anders was very impatient, so she pushed the button herself," continued Jack. "Radio acknowledged the distress call; asked James if he needed help. When Jillian cocked the hammer back on the revolver, James quickly acknowledged *yes*. Capt. John Schackelford was the first to respond. He then called out for everything we had. Soon after the cavalry arrived; radio called in SWAT. I'm not sure I know why," continued Caldwell, "but even several trucks from the fire department showed up. The paramedics, of course, were also there. Soon the entire complex looked like a flattened Christmas tree covered in blue, red, and yellow lights."

Jack then drank a long sip of water, easing a suddenly dry throat. He then went on. "The next thing that Miss Anders did was equally surprising. She asked James if he was married. He said he was; that he had a four-year-old son and another baby on the way. She asked if he loved his wife. James, of course, answered that he did love Barbara very much. About that time, I snuck around to the side of the building and could see James standing there with the revolver touching his forehead. I could only see Jillian Anders' hand, as she held the gun. Every once in a while, I could see that she was holding some kind of bottle in her left hand; and periodically she would raise it and lower it. I later found out, from James, that she was drinking Tequila, while her finger was on the trigger of the already cocked snub nose revolver. I also, later found out from James, that the barrel of the gun was so close that he could actually see a small red bead-like BB in the center of each hollow point bullet in the chamber."

"What was it?" asked Amy.

"They were explosive bullets," answered Jack. "Upon impact the bullet would explode and turn into a small grenade, which would guarantee maximum destruction to whatever it hit; mainly James Banner's head."

Amy Griner grimaced.

"After Miss Anders found out that James was married, she told him that since this is probably the last time that he'll talk to his wife, he should call her. James, of course, agreed and asked if he could come in and use her telephone. She laughed, continued to drink her tequila and said that she really did love his sense of humor, even in the face of death. Her voice was extremely cold and emotionless. She then reminded him that his radio was also a telephone, which only the detectives and uniformed supervisors possessed. We later were able to determine that her years as an emergency room nurse at Northside Hospital put her in direct contact with the uniformed officers and supervisors, which resulted in her acquiring a wealth of information about police operations."

Dr. Amy Griner was now sitting on the edge of her seat. "Did he call his wife?" she asked.

"He sure did," said Caldwell. "Once he told his wife what was happening, he was extremely surprised as to how calm she was. All she said was that everything was going to be okay. She told him not to worry; because God was still in control; and He would take care of him, and bring him safely home to her, and their son. She also said that she felt their baby's kick in her womb. Barbara Banner was truly a woman of faith, who totally trusted in Our Lord Jesus Christ. She confidently told her husband that this was God's battle, and there was a reason as to why this was happening. She then urged him to be patient and wait for God to tell him what he should do. She then told him how much she loved him and hung up."

"Did he, do it?" asked Amy.

"Yes, he did. He waited; and he waited. Just as she said."

"Well?" Amy asked in anticipation. "How long did he have to wait?"

"Exactly three hours and forty-five minutes!" answered Caldwell. "It was the longest three hours and forty-five minutes of my life." Jack Caldwell looked down and rubbed his forehead. "There were times, during that wait, when I wanted to jump up and put a bullet through her head; but James just put out his hand towards me; letting me know that he had it under control."

"Jack, how did it end?" Amy's voice was loud and strained.

"Just like Barbara had told him," Jack smiled. "To this day he swears that the words which came out of his mouth weren't his. They came from someone else. He did not realize that he was speaking them. They just blurted out." Jack swallowed hard. "'TELL ME ABOUT THOSE PICTURES YOU TOOK IN PARIS' was what he said. I heard him say it. Everyone around us heard him say it. Jillian even heard him say it; because she immediately reacted. She put down the gun, on a nightstand next to her; and she turned towards a fireplace in her bedroom. That's all it took. James followed by several other officers went through that window and immediately subdued her."

"What was it he said???" asked Amy, incredulously.

"He simply said, 'tell me about those pictures you took in Paris;' and that was it. I'll never forget those words. As long as I live, those words will be burned into my mind, forever."

"That's unreal?" Amy said with a look of total disbelief. "She was arrested, wasn't she?"

"Well, yes and no," Jack answered.

"What do you mean?" Amy's eyes were open wide. "She pointed a gun at a cop and threatened to kill him. Did she have to kill him first, in order to be arrested?"

"Calm down," said Jack, as he touched her hand. "We did arrest her that night; but James met her in court the next morning and asked the judge to dismiss all charges against her. Which the judge, reluctantly, did. The judge said that it was only because Banner was the primary victim that he was agreeing to dismiss the charges. He then told Miss Anders that she needed to get on her knees and thank God that she was not spending the next twenty years in prison."

"Why would he do such a thing?" asked Amy Griner.

"I honestly think that I and Chief Bobby Moore, who was a Captain at that time, are the only two who guessed the real reason," answered Caldwell. "James Banner wanted to save her. The same way he saved Clark Friday last week. That's why we call him 'the Minister'. It's his uncontrollable and inherent need to save people. Not just physically save them; which is also a strong desire of his; but also, their soul. As we walked out of the courtroom with Jillian Anders, because we were giving her a ride home, James whispered to me that he was going to sit in the backseat with her. I asked him if he wanted her to finish the job she started. He smiled and shook his head and said 'just trust me. I think I can introduce her to Jesus Christ; and He can save her.' I smiled and nodded, obligingly."

"Well, did he?" asked Amy.

"Five minutes, after we had gotten out of the parking lot; Jillian explained that she was at the very end of her rope and hanging on by an extremely thin thread. She honestly felt like a complete and total failure; especially after she got such a rotten performance evaluation; and she was sure to be fired. In fact, she, probably, already had been. She went on to say that the only good and beautiful thing she had ever done in her life were those pictures she took, while she was in Paris. She then looked over at James and said that she really did want to show them to him. She was sure that he would agree with her. When he answered that he would very much like to see them; she asked the question that Banner was waiting and praying that she would ask. 'Why did you ask me about those pictures' she asked him. She went on to say that Jim knew nothing about her or her life. How would he know about those pictures?"

Jack Caldwell looked directly into Dr. Amy Griner's eyes. "I don't know how strong your faith is Amy; or if you even believe in God ..."

"I'm a Christian!" Amy interrupted. "I very much believe in God and Jesus Christ, as my living Savior." She then took Jack's hand and said, "now continue."

"I'm glad we got that over with," smiled Jack. "Mainly, because, James said that the next words out of his mouth weren't his. God just took over. He told Jillian that there was Someone Who did know about her and her life. That Someone loved her very much; and wanted her to have an abundant and happy life. He asked if she wanted to meet Him? Of course, she responded with a loud 'OF COURSE I DO!', and that was all it took. After Banner told her, what you heard him tell Clark Friday, she accepted Jesus Christ as her living Savior; and she was saved."

"WOW!" exclaimed Amy. "Does this happen often to him?"

"Remind me to tell you, when you have time, about Henry Mackworth," answered Jack. "Then you'll understand why it does happen so often to him."

TWENTY-TWO

AFTER SIX MONTHS OF TESTIMONY, WHICH PRIMARILY INCLUDED the testimony of Henry Friday, a Federal Grand Jury, which was convened in the Atlanta Northern District, returned 461 indictments against 87 members of the Dixie Mafia. If convicted, it would virtually mean the complete destruction of that entire criminal organization of evil. The primary charges, which included murder and conspiracy to commit murder of a Federal Agent, namely Roberto Cardinal, stemmed from a law which was known as the Racketeer Influenced Corrupt Organizations Act, commonly known as the RICO statute. The penalties could include from 25 years to life, to the death penalty. The mandatory sentence, by law, however, had to be a minimum of 25 years of actual time in a Federal Penitentiary. That simply meant that the convicted felon would have to spend twenty-five years behind bars. Even a judge could not lessen the penalty. There was no such thing as "Good Time", or early release; or early parole. The inmates called it "Hard Time."

There were forty-eight indictments against Kirby Nox, and sixty-one indictments against Vernon Kimbrel.

"It looks like we have our work cut out for us," said Banner to the members of the Task Force. "Since we've all been deputized by the United States Attorney of the Northern District, it is our responsibility to assist the FBI and Federal Marshals in the round up of these animals."

"I know we all have personal and emotional feelings regarding this case," said Jack Caldwell; "but we have to consider the fact that we are professionals and we cannot let our emotions compromise this case in any way."

"I guess that means we can't give them what they deserve," yelled one of the agents. "We're not supposed to torture or kill them outright."

"Unless they really give us cause to do so," yelled another agent. Everyone laughed.

"As much as we would love to do that," said James Banner; "You're right. We have to bring them to justice. We will then let the government execute every one of their disgusting asses."

Five weeks of continuous surveillance and wiretaps proved to be very fruitful. Eighty-six of the fugitives had been arrested. The only two left were Kirby Nox and Vernon Kimbrel. It was believed that they had somehow fled to Mexico. If they were captured in Mexico, the only way to extradite them back to United States would be to agree not to give him the death penalty.

"There is no way we're going to agree to that," said James Banner to Tony Watson, the SAC of the Atlanta Bureau of the FBI.

"I'm afraid we have no choice," said Watson. "It's part of the treaty we have with Mexico."

"There's got to be another way," said Caldwell. "These guys are sociopaths. They are more than just a serial killers. One is the head of a violent and ruthless organized crime group; and the other is a merciless sociopathic serial killer, who takes great delight in torture and murder. They are absolute animals who have no regard for the law or human life. Plus, they have killed too many of our personal friends."

"Do we have to involve the Mexican government?" asked Amy Griner. "Both Nox and Kimbrel are American Fugitives. Why can't we just go down there and arrest them, and bring them back to the States?"

"Because that's kidnapping," said Watson. "I want to help you. I really do; but this is the worst time for the three of you to be asking me to do something like this. I have something extremely important that I want to do right now; and it's going to take every bit of courage and concentration I've got to pull it off."

"What in the world are you talking about?" asked Amy. "There couldn't be anything more important than capturing Kirby Nox and Vernon Kimbrel."

"Oh yes there is," said Watson as he opened his desk drawer and pulled out a small leather covered black box. He then got down on one knee. As he knelt in front of Amy Liner, he looked up and locked eyes with her.

"Oh, Tony!" she exclaimed. Tears began to run down her cheeks. She knew what was about to happen. "You're going to ask me to marry you?"

"Well, I'm absolutely sure not going to ask those two standing over there," he said looking at Jack and James.

Amy immediately laughed.

"Dr. Amy Griner, will you bless the rest of my life by becoming my wife for all eternity." Tears began to stream down his cheeks.

Amy's heart was skipping beats, her face covered with an angelic glow. "Yes! I will; but only on one condition."

Tony seemed a little shocked. "What kind of condition?"

"If you find a way for us to get Kirby Nox and Vernon Kimbrel, without the help of the Mexican authorities." Amy was smiling. She already knew what his answer would be.

"You already know that I would do anything for you."

Tony Watson jumped to his feet and grabbed Amy, pulling her close. Their kiss lasted nearly two minutes.

"Come on, you two," said Caldwell. "You have to either get a room, right now; or tell us how to get Nox and Kimbrel."

Both Watson and Griner could not help but laugh in mid-kiss.

"If I tell you how to do it, will the two of you leave us alone for the rest of the day?" said Watson. "After all we have a wedding to plan."

Amy's joyful smile sent a message unto itself.

"Absolutely!" said Banner.

Special Agent in Charge Tony Watson then explained how the FBI office in Mexico would assist them in the kidnapping of Kirby

Nox and Vernon Kimbrel. He also explained that it was done all the time, since the FBI hated dealing with the Mexican government on most fugitive situations. He went on to put them in contact with the DEA and United States Marshal's office, as well. They also committed several of their agents to assist in the apprehension of Nox and Kimbrel, if necessary. Tony Watson then assigned five of his best agents to go with Task Force members to Mexico, if they were needed, in an attempt to apprehend the two fugitives.

"You will virtually have a small army at your disposal," said Watson. "As I said, I would do anything for my future wife." He then kissed Amy again. "Now will the two of you please get out of my office."

Both Jack Caldwell and James Banner, smiling, turned and left the SAC's office.

"By the way," said Jack, as he opened the door, "congratulations!"

"Out!" said Tony and Amy at the same time.

Little did either Jack Caldwell or James Banner know that this was only the beginning of a very arduous and terrifying search for two of the most wanted men in America.

Twenty-Three

IT IS BELIEVED THAT A MAN'S STRONGEST POINT IS ESTABLISHED BY that which he loves the most. It is equally as obvious that his most vulnerable point is also defined by that which he loves the most. For Herman Friday, his dual points of strength and vulnerability were his beloved son, Clark. It was because of that reason that Friday was both totally confused and completely enraged when he received a phone call early that Sunday morning.

"Hi, Herman," said the sinister voice on the other end of the line. "I guess you know who this is."

"How did you get this number?" Friday asked.

"That's not important," said Kimbrel.

"It is to me," said Friday as he hung up.

When he told his FBI protection agents what was going on, a trace mechanism was immediately set up. As soon as the phone rang again, the agents locked in on the call.

"Okay," said Kimbrel, very calmly and arrogantly. "Since it's that important to you, I got the number from one of my police sources. Now can we talk?"

"What do you want, Vernon?" asked Friday.

"I want you to recant your testimony against me and Kirby Nox," responded Kimbrel. "I don't care about any of those others that you're testifying against. They can all rot in prison, as far as I'm concerned. All 85 of them. I just want you to forget about me and Kirby. Tell them you lied about us, and you never saw us do anything wrong. That's what I want! You spineless snitch."

"First, you dried up piece of snot, that will never happen; and secondly I want you to try to shut me up. You're nothing but a worthless coward, who's completely impotent. In other words, Vernon, you're not even a man. You're nothing more than a neutered animal."

To send Kimbrel into a spiral of venomous hatred, Herman Friday hung up once more.

The agents gave Herman a thumb up. They'd gotten the trace and had officers and agents on the way to his location, which was in Bremen, Georgia. Four minutes and forty-one seconds later Herman's phone rang again. The call was from the pay phone used by Kimbrel.

Everyone held their breaths. This time, however, the call came from one of the FBI agents.

"We found the pay-phone," said the agent, "but I'm afraid he's long gone. Put Major Banner on the phone."

"Major Banner," Jim said. "What do you have?"

"I'm afraid we missed him sir," the agent replied. "The way this guy stays one step ahead of us, sir; I think we have a mole in the department or even the task force."

"I tend to agree with you," said Banner. "Good work, agent. Your response time was fantastic. If you don't mind, I'd like you to canvass the area, in case someone may have seen or heard something. I also would appreciate it if you would bring in that pay-phone for evidence. We might be able to get something off of it, or even Kimbrel's prints off the coins he dropped in the phone."

"Will do, sir," said the agent as he hung up.

"It looks like he could have been tipped-off," Banner explained to the others "He knew we were coming. The agents at the scene of the call will canvas the area to see if anyone saw or heard anything."

"Thank you, sir," said the other agent, who was standing next to Friday. "I have to admit, Mr. Friday, that you handled yourself beautifully. In fact, you did a lot better than most of our veteran agents would have done, under the same circumstances."

"Thank you!" said Herman, very humbly. "That really means a

lot to me; especially coming from you." Herman Friday then did something that he had only done two other times. Once to James Banner and once to Dr. Amy Griner. He extended his hand in respect to the agent, who stood before him.

"I'm honored to shake your hand," said the Federal Officer, as he grasped Herman Friday's outstretched palm.

The agents immediately contacted their SAC, Tony Watson, who in turn contacted both Banner and Caldwell. Both Jack and James agreed to meet Watson and Amy at the safe-house where Friday was located. They arrived approximately forty-five minutes later. When Friday filled them in on what Kimbrel had said, Caldwell was livid.

"That total waste of humanity," said Caldwell; who was trying to cut down on his profanity, to be a better example to his men; as Amy had suggested.

"Can I call him a waste of humanity, also," said Friday. "I ain't got to impress anyone!"

They all laughed, including the three agents who were protecting Friday.

"We obviously have a mole somewhere," said Tony Watson. "I think that the best way to root him, or her, out is to start giving everyone assigned to the Task Force polygraphs."

"Let's not be so hasty," said Caldwell. "Doing something like that will cause a tremendous amount of distrust and destroy morale.

"I agree with Jack,'" said Amy. "I honestly can't believe that I actually agree with him; but I do."

Jack Caldwell winked at Dr. Griner.

"Don't get so cocky," she replied. "The only reason I agree with you is because the loss of morale among the task force members is a much greater loss than any benefit from the inaccuracy of the polygraph."

"That makes sense," said Watson. "Well does anyone have any idea as to what we can do?"

"I think I have an idea," said Herman Friday.

Everyone's jaw dropped. They had all forgotten that he was in the room. As they began to clumsily fumble for words, Amy Griner spoke up.

"What is your idea, Mr. Friday? I, for one, am very anxious to hear it."

"Thank you, Doctor Amy," said Friday. "Just give the snitch the wrong number. If Vernon calls it, then you got him."

Everyone looked at Friday. Was it outrageous?

"Herman, that's brilliant!" exclaimed Banner. "In fact, that is not only the simplest, but also, the most brilliant idea I have ever heard."

"Aren't you laying it on a little thick," Caldwell whispered to Banner.

Herman Friday overheard Caldwell. "Respect!"

Jack Caldwell, in turn, rolled his eyes.

"No, I'm being serious," said Banner. "Herman has the right idea. We simply narrow the field down to our most likely suspects; and that would mean those individuals who would have access or get access to Herman's private line." Caldwell looked around the room. "I feel certain that none of us would in any way endanger the case, or Herman, much less side with the likes of Kimbrel for any reason; so, I think we can rule each other out."

"Then let's get up whatever information we can; and get to work," said Tony Watson.

"Good grief," said Caldwell. "You have really gotten bossy, since you asked Amy to marry you!"

Banner, Amy and Tony all jumped at Jack at the same time, in an attempt to shut him up; but they were too late.

Herman Friday was the first to react. "What?" yelled Friday. "I can't believe your lowering your standards so much, that you're going to marry a cop. Dr. Amy, you could do so much better."

She immediately walked up to Herman and kissed him on the mouth.

"That's the nicest thing anyone has ever said to me, Herman. Thank you." she said with the biggest smile on her face.

"I can do a lot better than that," said Herman, "if you give me another kiss."

"Quit while your ahead," said Tony Watson, pulling Amy closer to him.

All three of the agents in the room started clapping their approval, as they congratulated the engaged couple.

Both Tony and Amy could only respond by smiling and blushing.

After going through all the files pertinent to the case, it was determined that only five people were suspects. They were Lieutenant Jammie Milford, Sergeant Theo Victor Smyth, Corporal Dewlap P. Hathaway, Sergeant Phillip P. Lockley, and Detective Hiram Masters.

"We now know how all five of these individuals got access to Herman's private line," said Banner. "All we have to do now is have five new lines put in, with five different numbers. We'll allow each of them to get access, in the same way, to each of the numbers. Then we simply wait. The number that Kimbrel calls will identify the mole. Just like Herman said."

"We'll have FBI techs install the new phones," said Caldwell. "That way we can maintain security and integrity."

"Thank you," said Tony Watson.

"No need to thank us," said Caldwell. "We're doing it because we trust Amy; and she has you by the testicles."

Everyone, including Herman Friday, burst into sudden laughter. They were laughing so hard they could barely hear Herman's phone ringing. They all abruptly stopped and immediately turned on the tracking devices. They then signaled for Herman to answer the phone.

"Who is this?" asked Friday.

"I guess you thought you'd never hear from me again," said Kimbrel. "Well, I have a surprise for you."

"What are you talking about?" asked Friday.

"Guess who I ran into, as he and his friends, were walking towards Piedmont park." He then put the pay phone against Clark Friday's mouth. "Say hello to your Daddy."

"Daddy," said Clark. "Don't do anything he asks. I'm going to be okay, Roberto told me so."

"Now are you ready to do what I want?" Kimbrel said, sadistically laughing.

"Don't you dare touch a hair on his head!" screamed Herman. "If you harm him, in any way, I swear that I'll slice you up piece by piece."

"Just for that, I think I'll begin by scalping this brat."

Suddenly, they could hear a scream; and the phone went dead. Herman was screaming into the phone yelling for his son.

"Marshal's Unit 90 to radio," split across the airways.

"That's one of Clark's protective detail," said Watson.

"Go ahead 90," radio responded.

"We're being shot at and I'm in foot pursuit of a suspect."

"Give us your location," said radio.

"I'm on fourteenth Street, running parallel to Piedmont Park."

"All units hold non-emergency traffic," said radio. "Any units available in the Piedmont Park area to assist Marshal's unit 90?"

So many units were attempting to respond, that it literally gridlocked the communication system.

"Unit one to radio," said Chief Bobby Moore, as he over-rode the 911 system. "Continue one or two units to an alley-way just west of the intersection of Fourteenth Street and Piedmont Road, across from the park."

"Radio received, Unit one." Radio responded. "Units 310 and 310B continue on call. All other units cancel."

"Start a signal four, right away," said the Chief. "I have a Federal agent, whose been shot in the neck. I'm giving him CPR at this time. Have someone from the Metro Task Force, also, start this way."

"I'm almost to you, Chief," said Banner as he slid up on the sidewalk next to Chief Moore.

Both Banner and Caldwell jumped out of their car. Then Watson and Griner pulled up behind them. The ambulance came screaming to a halt, as it came the wrong way down fourteenth street. The Chief then directed both police units to block all traffic.

"James," said Chief Moore. "I want you to immediately contact Herman; and let him know that his son is safe and unharmed and sitting in my car with Major Schackelford. We can't find Kimbrel. He took off running before he even saw us. He looked like he was running from a ghost. He was on that pay phone when we spotted him."

"What was he doing?" asked Caldwell.

"It honestly looked like he was trying to scalp the child, as he held the pay phone above his head," said Schackelford. "It was the strangest thing I've ever seen," said the Major. "Clark has to be the bravest young man I've ever met. He was just sitting there, calmly laughing at Kimbrel, and repeating, 'I told you that Roberto said that He was here to protect me.' Suddenly Kimbrel screamed and took off running."

"He screams like a girl," said Clark; "but he runs like the devil."

They all held back their laughter, out of respect for the wounded Marshal, who was now being transported to Grady Memorial Hospital. The second Marshal explained that they were distracted by what they thought were gunshots, which turned out to be cherry bombs, set off by a hippie, who said he was just playing a practical joke.

"Where's this hippie now?" asked Caldwell.

"I turned him over to one of the uniform units. They placed him under arrest for illegal fireworks and disorderly conduct. He was nineteen, so their taking him to the city jail."

"This sounds like a set-up," Caldwell said to the Chief.

"I agree," said Moore. "Unit one to radio."

"Go ahead, Sir," radio responded.

"Have the unit carrying the fireworks suspect, from Piedmont park, bring him to my location before he takes him to jail."

"Unit 322 B received. I'm on my way to you, Chief."

"Radio's clear, 322 B."

The second Marshal went on to explain that after he turned over the hippie to the uniformed officer, he looked back and could see his partner bleeding from what appeared to be his head, he also noticed that Clark was gone. That was when he called for help.

"You did the best you could," said Chief Bobby Moore. "Now head over to Grady and check on your partner."

"I will," answered the Marshal. "Thank you, Chief. Thank you for finding the kid and saving my partner's life."

Bobby smiled. "It's all in a day's work."

After the Marshal left, Bobby looked at both his cop and his minister. He stared at them for almost thirty seconds.

"What is it, Chief?" Banner finally asked.

"I am so jealous of you two. I prayed that I could experience what you two go through, just for one day. Now that I got my wish, I realize how much I miss it. Don't either one of you ever become Chief until you absolutely have to."

He then looked at them with pure admiration; and turned towards Major Schackelford.

"Johnny," said the Chief, "when you're Chief, they'll be your responsibility. Promise me that you will take care of them."

Major Schackelford smiled. "That will be a long time from now, Chief; but you do have my word."

"That's all I need!" Booby Moore then looked at James Banner and said, "Now get this young man to his daddy."

"I'm going to see my daddy." Clark's voice was filled to the brim with pure joy.

"Well that's the Chief of Police; and he gave us an order to do just that," said Caldwell. "So, yes, you are going to see your daddy."

"He is so thankful that you're okay," said Banner.

"I told him that Roberto said that 'He was going to take care of me'," Clark said with absolute confidence; "and He did. Daddy should not have worried at all."

"That's something we'll talk about, after we see your daddy," said James Banner. "Right now, how about if we get you an ice cream cone; and have the agents at your dad's place order some dinner for all of us."

"That is the best idea I have heard all day," said Clark. "You're a smart man, Major Banner."

"What about me," asked Caldwell, "don't you think that I'm also a smart man?"

"Well, your kinda smart, Major Jack," Clark answered in a voice of pure innocence.

James Banner bit his lip to keep from laughing.

"I'll have Major Schackelford contact you," said Chief Moore; "after we talk to that hippie with the fireworks."

"Thank you, Chief!" They all said in unison, as they pulled away.

Twenty-Four

As soon as they arrived at the safe house and were about to deliver Clark to his father, Banner received a radio transmission from Major Schackelford, asking him to call.

"Right away, Sir," Banner answered.

When they arrived, Herman's Friday's face lit up like the morning star. He wrapped his arms around his son, lifted him to his shoulders, and held him close. He did not want Clark to see the tears streaming down his face.

"Daddy! You're crying," said Clark.

"I know, son."

"But why?"

"Because I thought he was hurting you; and I couldn't get to you to protect you."

"But, Daddy," Clark said, as he pushed away to see his daddy's face, "I told you that Roberto told me that He would protect me."

Herman Friday's face changed to fear and confusion. "I don't understand," he said, looking directly into Clark's eyes, "Roberto is dead!" Herman then scanned the room to see if anyone had any different information.

"I know he's dead," said Clark. "He did not mean that he was going to save me. He told me that Jesus, who was with him, would save me; and He did!"

Herman Friday had a panicked looked on his face. He was beginning to sweat and was becoming very pale. He held out Clark towards Amy Griner, who rushed in and grabbed him. Herman immediately fell to his knees, and covered his face with his hands, and wept out loud. Amy immediately rushed Clark into another room, as she explained to him that everything was alright; and it was not his fault that his daddy was crying.

"I can't believe what I've done!" Friday wailed, "What have I done! What have I done!" His sobs became louder; and he began to beat the floor with his fists. "How could I have possibly killed such a man? What kind of animal am I? Why would he save my son, after what I did to him?"

James Banner rushed to his side and put his arm around Herman. Tears began to well up in Banner's eyes. They then flowed freely down his cheeks. His heart went out to this man, who was in pure agony.

"You have to listen to me, Herman," Banner said. "You can be forgiven. God's love is greater than any sin you have ever committed."

Friday bolted upright and looked directly into the minister's eyes. "There is no way, on earth, that God could ever forgive me for what I've done!" Friday said, through clenched teeth. "It's not just the number of people I've killed," he said, turning away from Banner's gaze, "it's the way I killed them. No one, not even God can forgive that!!!"

Banner turned Friday's face towards his own and held it there. He then locked his gaze onto Herman's eyes.

"Listen to your own son!" He said, emphatically. "In spite of his age; and in spite of his innocence; he holds the truth in his heart. He knows what God and Jesus Christ can do. He saved him, and He can save you."

Friday looked at the minister and his heart began to soften.

"James," Caldwell called out. "James, it's Major Schackelford. He needs to talk to you."

"Go," said Friday in a very calm voice. "We'll finish this conversation when you're done." He then put his arms around banner and embraced him. "You're a good man," he whispered in his ear.

Johnny Schackelford explained to Banner that the 'fireworks hippie' finally told them that Kimbrel had given him $50.00 to set off the fireworks 'as a prank.' He and the Chief felt like he was telling the truth after they threatened him with conspiracy to murder a federal marshal. He also informed him that the Marshal that was wounded was in stable condition and was expected to make a full recovery.

"Thank you, Major," said Banner; "at least there's some good news that came out of this mess."

"We have got to find this mole," Schackelford emphasized. "I and the Chief know that you are doing everything you can; but that child's not going to be safe until we identify him. The Chief wanted me to let you know that you not only have his total support; but you have unlimited resources to get this done."

"Thank you, sir," said Banner. "We have a plan in place, and we will get it done."

"May God bless and care for you and your task force," said Schackelford, as he hung up.

Clark had come back into the room and was wiping his daddy's tears from his eyes. In between wipes he would kiss his daddy's cheeks and whisper in his ear.

"My kisses will take away your tears," Clark said with a smile.

Herman looked up at the minister and nodded.

TWENTY-FIVE

IT TOOK NINE DAYS AND FIVE SEPARATE TELEPHONES, TO ESTABLISH, implement, and set the plan in motion to identify the mole in the police department, who was providing Vernon Kimbrel with the information he needed. It was Dr. Amy Griner's knowledge of human nature that helped the most in the implementation of the plan.

Herman Friday was moved to a new safe-house. Clark was secretly moved to the same safe-house with his daddy. Only key task force members knew the location and only key task force members knew his new telephone number. All five suspects were allowed to obtain one of the bogus numbers in the same way that they had originally obtained the old number. The plan seemed like a long shot, because it was filled with unforeseen variables.

"It will take a miracle for this plan to work," said Tony Watson; "but it's the best plan we have."

"Occasionally, one of the suspects would call the number just to test it out. They would call under the guise of checking on Herman. The fact that Herman would answer seemed to give them confidence in the number.

"Well, as long as we're just sitting here waiting," said Amy to Jack, "Why don't you tell us about Henry Mackworth, as you promised?"

"You don't forget anything, do you?" said Caldwell. "Well, it happened to Jim. Let's have him tell the story."

"I guess we have plenty of time to kill," said Banner, as he nodded and agreed to tell the story. "Henry Mackworth was a Metro Police

Officer in Washington, D.C. In my opinion," Banner continued, "he was also a sociopath. While I was in the military, assigned to the Criminal Investigation Division at Ft. Belvoir, Virginia, my wife convinced me to take her on a day trip to see the Capital and the White House. I reluctantly agreed."

"On our way, there we came to a street that was oval shaped," Banner continued.

"Oh yeah," said Watson. "That's where the Smithsonian, the Aero-Space Museum, and …"

"I want to hear the story, Tony," Amy interrupted, pushing Watson's arm. "I don't want a guided tour of Washington, DC!"

"Sorry," said Tony Watson, turning bright red.

"The traffic was grid-locked as we were circling the oval, looking for a place to park," Banner said. "I noticed that there was a police car next to my car; and we were in the same predicament. We were both in the middle of the intersection, blocked in by stalled traffic both in front of us and behind us. We sat there and watched the light change from green to yellow, and then to red, as we began to pull forward. At that time, officer Mackworth turned on his red lights, and gave a short blast on his siren. He then motioned for me to pull over."

"What for?" Watson interrupted, again.

"That was my exact question," said Banner. "Mackworth said that I had run a red light. My wife, Barbara, reminded him that he was right beside us and he also ran the light. He told her to keep quiet and not to obstruct justice, or he would have to arrest her."

"What an ass-hole!" said Dr. Amy Griner.

"Now who's interrupting," quipped Watson. He regretted it the moment he said it, when he saw the look on Amy's face.

"Please continue, Jim." Watson said with a sheepish look on his face.

"Well, it gets worse," Banner continued. "When I tried to explain to him, that I was an Atlanta police officer, on military leave and I was presently a criminal investigator with the Army; he simply laughed. He then stated that he doesn't ever go to Atlanta because the crime rate was too high; and he hates the military. He then advised me that he was giving me a ticket because I disregarded the red light. I decided not to argue with him, since it was obvious that it would do no good. He then told me to follow him to the police precinct, since I was under arrest. I was shocked, but I got into my car and followed him."

"The precinct was only a couple of blocks away. When we got there, he handed my driver's license to the desk Sergeant and explained to him what happened. The sergeant looked even more shocked than me and I heard him ask Mackworth 'why did you arrest him and give him a ticket for something that was obviously unavoidable?' Mackworth answered that it was a collar; and he wanted credit for it. The sergeant then agreed with what Amy said and told him that he was a disgrace to the badge and to get out of his precinct. The sergeant was very apologetic and told me that the bond was $10.00, and that would include the fine. He also said that I did not have to return to any court appearance, unless I wanted to do so. I paid the $10.00, got my license and the sergeant stamped the ticket 'PAID IN FULL'. I then left. Henry Mackworth had, obviously, ruined our day-trip to the Nation's Capital."

"That's a horrible story," said Amy. "I hope I never run into that person."

"That's not the whole story," said Jack. "The ending was a miracle."

Amy looked wide-eyed, as she looked directly at Banner. "Then please go on."

"It was almost three years later," Banner continued. "I had gotten out of the military and went back to the Atlanta Police Department. Whenever I would leave home, and go to work, in my patrolman's uniform, my wife would always tell me to be a good cop and not one like Henry Mackworth. She also had reminded me on several occasions, that God had a purpose in allowing Henry Mackworth to do what he did. She then would say that God's timing is not the same as ours. Little did I know that God's purpose would begin on that November evening, when I would be patrolling a beat in Southwest Atlanta."

Both Amy Griner and Tony Watson moved a little closer to Major James Banner, in order to hear every word.

"It was about 8:00 pm and I was patrolling down Ashby Street, in South West Atlanta. I the saw a Ford Crown Victoria, Black in color, with Washington DC plates run a stop sign at Ashby and Lee. They almost hit another vehicle and were driving very erratic."

Dr. Amy Griner held her hand to her mouth, and blurted out, "You've got to be kidding me!!! Was it him?"

Special Agent Tony Watson put his hand on her shoulder and calmly said, "Let him finish, angel."

"As I walked up to the car," Banner went on to say, "I noticed that the driver was holding his badge, outside of his rolled down window. I then told him that I needed to see his driver's license; as I stood behind the driver's side of the vehicle. He responded by asking me if I was going to show him any 'police courtesy', just like they did in Washington DC'. His speech was slurred, and he reeked of alcohol. When I told him that I thought that he said he never came to Atlanta, he looked at me, and squinted his eyes. He then became as pale as a ghost as the blood drained from his face and he threw up. He recognized me."

"WOW!" Amy blurted out. "I would have loved o have been there!"

"I then asked him to step out of the vehicle," Banner continued.

"You did arrest him, didn't you?" Amy interrupted, again.

"Amy, you're getting ahead of yourself," Jack Caldwell said. "Let him finish."

"He looked very humiliated and ashamed," Banner went on to say. "He told me that his partner was a 'tea totter' and was his 'designated driver.' He then begged me to let him take the car, instead of impounding it, since it was a city vehicle."

Dr. Amy Griner then opened her mouth and started to speak when Tony Watson put his hand over it and stopped her.

"I didn't even acknowledge his request, much less, respond to it," Banner said. "I simply had him turn around, while I searched and handcuffed him. That was when he started to cry. He went on to say he was stupid, when he gave me that ticket; and he should not have done so. After all, the desk Sergeant went on to change it to a simple traffic violation, with a fine of only $10.00. I told him that his desk sergeant was a good man, and if he were here I would have no problem with turning him loose. Now, however, he had to face the consequences of his own actions. He was now sobbing uncontrollably and begging for mercy. He said he was going to lose his job, his family, and everything he had ever worked for. It was at that time that his partner stepped out of the vehicle and asked me if he could try to talk some sense into officer Mackworth. I allowed him to do so. He told Henry that he was making a complete fool out of himself. He also said that Henry was a narcistic sociopath who was totally self-center, and he knew it. Maybe now he would fully understand that there are consequences for his actions. His partner's name was Jake Morrow. At that moment in time, I really liked the guy. He was straight forward, honest, and down to earth."

"I'm sure he was exactly like your partner," Jack quipped.

James only smiled. "I asked Detective Morrow if he had a driver's license. He acknowledged that he did; and showed it to me. I then asked him to sit in the driver's seat of his city vehicle. He thanked me; and did as I requested. I then put Henry in the back seat of my patrol vehicle, while he was still handcuffed. I kept his gun, badge and ID card, and driver's license up front with me. His sobbing had calmed, but he continued to choke-up, every now and then. He stated that this was going to cost him his job. I responded with a very cold tone that I figured it would. He also said that it would cost him his marriage. I responded again by saying that when he arrested me in Washington, it did ruin the day for my wife and I, but it didn't cost us our marriage. I then put salt into an open wound when I told him that my wife and I believed in each other, and our Lord, Jesus Christ. No matter how despicable he was on that afternoon, it made us stronger; and it made me a better cop. I told him that he was the worst cop I had ever met in my entire life; but my wife and I prayed for him every week. We asked God to cause him to become a better person; and to help us learn from the evil he showed towards us."

Amy looked at Banner, with tears in her eyes; as Tony Watson held her closer to him. "It's a lesson we could all learn," Watson whispered to her. Amy looked at her future husband and smiled.

"I finished writing the citations. I then stepped out of my patrol car; and opened the back door. Mackworth was in shock, especially when I told him to step out of my vehicle. He reluctantly did so. He was even more shocked when I took off his handcuffs; and handed him his copies of the three citations. They were for Driving under the Influence of alcohol, Reckless driving, and disregard of a stop sign. His eyes welled up with tears, once again, but this time I'm sure they were for a far different reason. He read what I had written across the front of each ticket. It said PAID IN FULL BY OUR LORD JESUS CHRIST!"

"Oh! That is so beautiful!!" Amy replied. "What did you do then?"

"I called over Detective Morrow, and I returned officer's Mackworth's gear to him. I then told him to get him back to his hotel safely. I also advised him that there would be no charges against him. I then looked at officer Mackworth, who had tears streaming down his face, as he asked me why. I simply replied that Our Lord, Jesus Christ, gave me a chance for eternal life; and now He's giving you a chance for the same thing. That was the last I ever saw of Henry Mackworth."

"So, what happened to him?" Watson and Griner asked together.

"That's the best part," said Jack. "Do you have the letter, and the newspaper articles?"

"They're in my desk at home," Banner answered.

"Just tell them what happened," Caldwell said.

Banner nodded. "It was a couple of years later when I got a letter from officer Henry Mackworth. In that letter, he thanked me for everything I had done for him. In fact, he said that everything that happened that night did not cost him his job, it caused him to be a much better cop and got him a promotion to Sergeant; and he absolutely thanked me for that. It also did not cost him his marriage, which was basically on the rocks, long before he went to Atlanta, it revived it and made it stronger than ever. He also absolutely thanked me for that. He went on to say that he also found Our Lord, Jesus Christ, to be his Lord and Savior; and he thanked God for that and the words on that ticket. I read those words PAID IN FULL BY OUR LORD JESUS CHRIST every morning, when I start my day; and my wife and I pray for you and your family, officer Banner."

"What an amazing story," said Tony Watson; "but what about the newspaper articles?"

"There was an article in the Washington Post about two years later, which acknowledged a certain Washington DC Police Sergeant, named Henry Mackworth, who was donating his time to juveniles, in the inner city, in a big-brother mentoring program. The Post also stated that Sgt. Mackworth was single handedly responsible for leading hundreds of young people to become involved in church events, the scouts, and numerous other community activities. I also know for a fact, and another newspaper article, that Henry was teaching a bible study class for law enforcement officers; and he was able to lead over three hundred officers and their families to our Lord, Jesus Christ, as their Savior. That article was Sergeant Henry Mackworth's obituary. About four and a half years after the initial Post article came out he had a heart attack, while he was coaching an inner-city basketball team, and died. It was later determined that his earlier life of alcoholism had seriously damaged his heart and liver."

The room fell into shock. Dr. Amy Griner looked directly at Major James Banner, as her tears began to form. She then turned to Special Agent in Charge Tony Watson, her future husband, and buried her head in his shoulder and cried like a baby. Tony Watson could not hold back his own tears. Both he, and his future wife, held on to each other as tears flowed down their cheeks.

"My wife and I attended his funeral," said Banner. "His wife had asked me to be a pall-bearer. She also asked my wife and I to sit with the family. It was the biggest funeral I had ever seen. The news media estimated over twenty thousand attendees. They had to install numerous speakers outside to accommodate the thousands who could not fit into the church."

James Banner paused in order to wipe a tear from his eye. He then swallowed and looked up.

"I'll never forget what his wife said as she, herself delivered the eulogy," Banner said.

. "She had to be an unbelievably courageous woman." exclaimed Amy "I'm sorry, Tony, but I could never do that at your funeral."

Tony Watson nodded, squeezing her hand.

"She was both brave and courageous," acknowledged Banner, as he continued. "Janel, Henry Mackworth's wife, spoke slowly, but she was extremely articulate. Her words were mesmerizing. She told the story of the first encounter I had with her husband. She referred to him as her 'first husband', the man she was about to divorce. She went on to describe our second encounter, as well as, his reaction, when he returned home, to the police citations I had issued to him the night before. She read each of the three tickets. When she started to read what I had written across each citation, she broke down. She fell to her knees and wept uncontrollably. The pastor gently lifted her, and led her to his seat, behind the podium. The pastor then read the words on the citations, himself. It says, 'PAID IN FULL BY OUR LORD JESUS CHRIST.' The pastor then paused to wipe a tear from his own eye. He then noticed that Janel was standing next to him. He returned the tickets to her and stepped back to his seat. She then looked directly at me and wiped both of her eyes, as she said that only the Lord God Almighty could have directed you to write those words Lieutenant Banner. It's because of your courage and commitment to follow the words of Our Lord Jesus Christ that Henry and I remained married; but he became my second husband. He became a man of God. He became a Christian. He then asked me the most beautiful question I had ever heard. Amy was on the edge of her seat; as were the church attendees at Henry's funeral that day. He asked me if I would be willing to renew our vows in a Christian church, with a Christian pastor; and we could become a Christian husband and a Christian wife. She then said I held him so tight and kissed him so many times, and cried so hard, that I'm not sure if I ever answered him. She then smiled, and the church broke out in laughter; and the thousands outside did the same."

Tony Watson was a tough agent. But his toughness gave way as he listened to each word of the Henry Mackworth story. He simply pulled Amy closer to him, and they both let their tears flow down their cheeks.

"Janel," Banner continued, "locked eyes with me once more. She drank some water and said that she felt like she was a very strong Christian. She said that she had grown up in a Christian home and went to church almost every Sunday. She honestly felt that when she first married Henry, almost 27 years ago, that she would be able to someday lead him to the Lord. No matter how hard I prayed, it did not happen. She then exclaimed, 'I'm mad at you, Lieutenant Banner,' she spoke with sincere emotion. 'I tried for 18 years to get through to that stubborn and hard-headed man; but he never listened; until I told him that I wanted a divorce. That was when he volunteered to go to Atlanta to interview some witnesses to a murder in Washington. That was also when he met you. You were able to accomplish with eight words, which were written on a traffic citation, what I had not been able to do in eighteen years. That's why I'm mad at you James Banner; and that's why,' she then looked at my wife, "I will continue to pray, and thank God for you and your family; and always love you for the remainder of my time on earth. Then I'll await the day that Henry and I can both thank you in heaven, along with the hundreds of people that Henry led there. All because of your eight words'. Her tears came down in buckets, as she held out her arms to me. My tears almost caused me to trip, as I ran up the stairs to the podium, to grab her. I guess you never really know what's going to happen at a funeral; but the moment I embraced Janel, both inside the church and outside the church the people erupted with applause."

TWENTY-SIX

AFTER FIVE AND A HALF DAYS OF WAITING, IT WAS BEGINNING TO look like the plan had failed. It was three o'clock in the afternoon when one of the bogus phones rang.

"Hello," said Herman.

"I guess you now realize that I'll always be able to find you and your kid; and there's nowhere that you can hide," said Vernon Kimbrel.

"How did you get this number," said Friday, with a huge grin on his face; as he held his son and looked at the four people around him; and pointed to the phone.

Watson and Griner just shook their heads.

Caldwell clenched his fist and whispered, "I knew it!"

Banner looked down, in disgust.

Then they all smiled; knowing that they had discovered the mole.

"I know where your kid is," Kimbrel said. "This time I'm not going to kidnap him. I'm just plain going to kill him. You can only stop me, by calling me on this burner beeper, which will let me know that you're not going to testify." He then laughed his familiar sadistic laugh and hung up.

Herman hung up the phone and smiled, as he looked at Clark who was in the living room of the safe-house, watching TV and supposedly doing his homework at the same time.

"I knew Masters was a real scum bag," said Caldwell; "but I never would have believed that he could be this evil."

"He actually could be held responsible for many of Kimbrel's killings," said Watson. "All we need to do is show that he was helping Kimbrel when he committed the murders."

"Let's advice Chief Moore, immediately," said Banner; "and get that crook, with a badge, indicted as soon as possible."

"We may be acting from emotions and not from logic and reason," said Dr. Amy Griner.

"What are you talking about," snapped Caldwell. "He has been telling a cold-blooded serial killer all of our moves. He needs to be stopped, immediately."

"I agree," said Amy; "but he needs to be stopped correctly and for good; and we can do exactly that." She then looked directly at Tony Watson and smiled, as she said, "we need to catch him in the act; and have everything recorded."

Watson's eyes slightly widened, as he looked up at her. A smile then crossed his face and lit up as he suddenly realized what she was saying.

"Amy's right," said Watson. "Right now, we have very little with which to charge Masters, much less convict him. If we take what we now know, however, and use it to our advantage, we can probably nail him on everything, including murder and the RICO statute."

"I'm all for it," said Banner; "but exactly how are we going to do that?"

"It won't be simple," said Watson; "and we'll need Herman's help."

"I'm way ahead of you," said Herman Friday who was listening from the other room. "You're going to have to move me again, and Masters will probably do it. I'll take it from there. Just tell me what information you want leaked."

"You'll not only have to leak information," said Amy, "but you will also have to have him call you at a strange hour, when we know he'll be off duty; and we can determine which telephone he uses."

"I can handle that," Friday assured them.

Amy then looked at Tony. "You, my darling, have to use your financial skills to determine where Masters keeps his money; and you have to make sure that it disappears."

"All my years as a financial fraud investigator and accountant are about to pay off," said Tony, very proudly.

"You, my dear friend," she said, looking at Jack Caldwell, "have to arrange to get Hiram Masters suspended from the police department; and eliminate any means of income for about one month."

"I'm sure I can do that," answered Caldwell. "Can I involve the Chief?"

"Of course, you can," said Amy; "as well as, Major Schackelford; but no one else, unless you check with us first."

"You got it," Jack replied.

"What about me?" asked Banner. "Do I have a job?"

"You'll have the most important job of all," said Amy, with a smile. "You will be my 'go to' boy."

"What!!!" Banner blurted out.

"You will help me in setting up all surveillance on Masters," Amy answered. "We need to know what he's doing 24 hours a day, for the duration of this thing."

"That sounds more like it," said Banner.

It took nearly three days to get the entire plan scripted and ready to go. Tony Watson, along with several close friends in the financial investigation division were able to determine that Hiram Masters had four bank accounts in three different counties in the State of Georgia; and one Savings and Loan account in the State of Tennessee; and all were ready to be frozen, as if they had been illegally compromised and drained. The total amount of money involved was over nine hundred thousand dollars.

Jack Caldwell had tipped off a close friend of both his and Jim Banners, who was a television news reporter, of an upcoming DUI sting operation. Caldwell had also arranged for a very reliable informant, who's life Caldwell had saved, to take on the role of a drunk driver.

James Banner had called upon his close friend Captain Jerod Spence, the Commander of the Atlanta Police Department's Special Operations Division to provide the vehicles and manpower for an around the clock surveillance of Hiram Masters and any of his contacts. Spence promised Banner unlimited resources and person-power since his division consisted of both men and women.

Herman Friday had gone over his script more than twenty times, until he could virtually recite it in his sleep.

On the fourth day, the execution of Dr. Amy Griner's plan began with a telephone call from Major Johnny Schackelford to Sgt. Hiram Masters. Schackelford asked Masters to assist in the top secret move of Herman Friday, and his son Clark, to a different safe house. Masters seemed somewhat surprised, until Schackelford played on his narcissistic nature and told him that he had proven himself to be very reliable and honest in his past dealings with Herman Friday; and the Chief wanted him to be permanently assigned to the duty of Friday's mobile transfer security.

A huge smile came over Masters' face. He even puffed out his chest a little.

"I'll take care of it," said Masters. "I suppose you and the Chief realize, by now, that I have changed for the better?"

Schackelford bit his lip to keep from laughing out loud over the phone. "Of course, we do," said Schackelford. "Both the Chief and I see you for the true person you are, Hiram, by your very notable behavior for the past several months. You truly are an amazing individual."

"Thank you, Johnny," Masters said, thinking that he was now on the same level as the major. "I won't disappoint you or the Chief."

"I'm sure you won't," Schackelford answered. "Captain Jerod Spence will bring you all of the details on the move. It will be in a top secret envelop, which will be marked for your eyes only. Spence knows that, despite the rank difference, he, and his men. Are to answer to you in this operation. He may not like it, but you will be in charge." Schackelford deliberately paused for the entire concept to sink into Masters' already bloated head. "Can you work under those circumstances?" Schackelford asked.

Sgt. Hiram Masters' face was beaming with a smile that literally showed every single one of his yellow teeth. "Don't worry, Johnny," he said once more, which caused Shackleford's face to become bright red with anger. "I can handle Jerod Spence. Remember he used to work for me when he was a 'wet-behind-the-ears' useless patrolman. I think he'll remember that I taught him everything he knows." Masters arrogance was becoming more and more bold; which was exactly what Amy Griner had hoped would happen.

After Major Schackelford hung up, he looked directly at Chief Moore and said, "that is the most arrogant and self-centered human being I have ever talked to!"

"That's exactly what we planned on," said Moore. "His arrogance and narcissism are his two most dependable characteristics."

Both Major Johnny Schackelford and Chief Bobby Moore then laughed.

That night Hiram Masters logged on to his home computer to perform his routine of "checking his money." He loved doing that. It gave him a new sense of respectability.

"If only they knew how rich I really am!" He said to himself. "One of these days they'll find out; but by then, I'll be long gone, vacationing off some Caribbean Island."

Suddenly his heart skipped a beat. The first account showed $2.18.

"What's happening?" He said out loud.

The second account showed less than $1.00. He was near heart attack level. The third and fourth accounts showed zero dollars. Masters grabbed his chest and let out a string of obscene curse words enough to make a sailor blush. The Savings and loan account was also empty. Hiram Masters did the only thing he could do at 1:00 am. He drank himself to sleep, with his gun next to his head, contemplating pulling the trigger.

Being the absolute narcissist that he was, he woke up the next morning, still alive, with the gun still there.

"What am I going to do?" He said out loud. He jumped up and threw the gun back on the bed. His eyes were filled with crooked red lines, which marked the many broken blood vessels, which he had endured during the night. "What am I going to do?" He repeated. He then put his hands over his face and bawled like a baby.

The misery of that morning was suddenly interrupted by the

ringing of his phone. At first, he thought about not answering it. He then looked at the clock, which he forgot to set. It was already 10:00 am; and he was supposed to be at his desk by 7:00 am to meet Capt. Jerod Spence.

"Oh, no!" he said, as he picked up the phone.

"Sgt. Masters," said Spence. "Are you okay?"

"Of course, I am!" said Masters. "I'm sorry, Jerod; but I had a rough night last night. That's why I'm so late."

"No problem, sir," said Spence, playing on Masters arrogance. "If it's a concern over the money that's got you worried," Spence said, and paused, knowing exactly what the problem really was, "then stop worrying."

Masters turned pale white and he almost passed out.

"The chief has signed off on unlimited resources for this operation." Spence took great delight in knowing that Masters, the crooked cop, was going out of his mind.

"Great," said Masters. "That did concern me some. I'm going to take a shower, and I'll be in shortly." He said as he hung up.

Jerod Spence immediately called Major Banner and told him what happened.

"I guess everything is going as planned," said Banner. "Good work, Jerod. How are you holding up?"

"I guess you realize that the worst part of this assignment," said Spence, "is pretending that I'm showing that worthless piece of crap, who is a criminal, and who carries our badge, both honor and respect."

"I know how you feel. Jerod. Believe me. I do." Said Banner. "We both had to do it for years; for no other reason, than he out-ranked us. Now, however, we have a purpose for all of this. Soon the whole country will see that Hiram Masters is a man totally without honor or respect. A bright light will be shown on his true evil."

"By the way," said Spence. "Watson must have really come through with getting rid of Masters' money. He sounded like he was totally bent out of shape and still drunk. He must have found out last night."

"Well, it sounds like everything is going as planned!" smiled Banner. "Dr. Amy Griner is pure genius!"

"She sure is!" acknowledged Captain Jerod Spence.

Twenty-Seven

It was almost 12:00 noon before Masters arrived to meet with Capt. Spence. Spence looked at his watch.

"Sorry, I'm a little late," said Masters, irritated by the gesture; "but it was a rough night, as I said."

"I understand," said Spence.

"I really don't care if you do or don't understand," Masters blurted out, letting his old ugly side burst forth. "Remember, Spence, I'm the one who's running this operation!"

"Yes, you are," said Jerod Spence, very professionally. "You are, because I recommended you for it. I felt like we could work together, because I respect you very much. We didn't see eye to eye on a lot of things, but I always respected you." Spence bit his lip and swallowed hard to keep from throwing up. "Now do we work together; or do I tell Major Shackleford that I want out, because you are not the person I thought you were?"

Masters looked at Spence with disgust, but he knew he had to work with Spence or lose this golden opportunity. He might even have a shot at replacing some of his mysteriously missing money.

"You're right," said Masters, gritting his teeth. "I got some bad news last night concerning my daughter," said Masters. "I hear she's back on drugs. You have to forgive me for being somewhat ill tempered."

"I completely understand," said Spence, shaking his head as if in commiseration. "So, can we start all over, with different attitudes?"

"I can, if you can," Masters spoke like a high-school juvenile.

When Spence stuck out his hand, Masters reluctantly took it.

"Well, here's the envelop for your eyes only, sir." Spence handed it to him and walked away.

Masters slowly walked into his office and slowly opened the envelope, locking the door behind him. According to his orders from the chief, he was to arrange for a top-secret transportation of Herman Friday, and his son, Clark, from their present safe house to a new location that would be divulged on Monday morning. The most difficult part of the operation was the fact that it had to be done so quickly. The move had to be completed by noon that same day, in order to protect the secrecy of the entire operation. Masters bought it, hook, line, and sinker.

That afternoon Masters spent hours contacting his bankers and his savings and loan offices, in an effort to find out what happened to his money.

"Aren't you supposed to verify the information," Masters screamed into the phone, "before you do something like that." He was being told the same story here that he'd been told by each one. Essentially, they had received his letter transferring his money to his off-shore account, which he told them he would do very soon. They also told him that once the money was transferred, as his requested in the letter, the account number, which was in a separate envelop, was destroyed. It was then deleted from their computers.

"I did as I was instructed," said the manager of each financial institution. "It was your signature on the letter; and all of the forms were correctly filled out and signed by you. They were all in your hand writing. You have to admit, Mr. Masters, you do have a very distinctive hand writing."

"Well, I didn't do it!" Masters yelled. "So, how do I get my money back? Aren't you supposed to replace it? Aren't you insured for something like this."

"Yes! We are insured for matters of fraud or theft," said the manager; "but this does not fit any of those."

"Then, how do I get my money back," Masters screamed into the phone.

His call was interrupted by a sharp knock at the door. "Just a minute!" he yelled. "I'm on a private call."

"Then hang-up!" said Chief Bobby Moore, in a very sharp and irritated voice.

Masters immediately hung up; and unlocked the door.

"What are you doing, locking your door," yelled the Chief; "and what is all of your screaming and yelling about. Everyone in the squad room can hear you."

"I'm so sorry, sir," Masters said, scrambling for words, through a very blurred and hung-over brain. He then saw the letter 'for his eyes only'. "I locked the door in order to read this very confidential letter, which you wrote for my eyes ... I mean, these eyes"

"Sgt. Masters! Are you drunk?" The Chief yelled. "No sir, I am not," Masters said. "I did have a few drinks, last night; because I had some very depressing news about my daughter being on drugs. I also did not get much sleep; but I am okay, sir."

Chief Moore looked at him; and knew that he was lying; but decided for the plan's sake; he would let it go.

He then shut the door behind him. "Well, did you read the contents in the letter; and can you accomplish what I want."

"Is the Pope Catholic?" Masters answered in his usual arrogance.

"I want a yes or no answer, Masters!" The Chief snapped. "I don't want any childish clichés. Is this something that you can handle?"

"Yes, sir," said Masters, in an attempt to gain composure. "I can assure you that Captain Spence and I will get this done, exactly as you requested. We'll bet our jobs on it."

Chief Bobby Moore nodded; but he could not resist one final jab at Masters' arrogance.

"Capt. Jerod Spence was the one who actually recommended you for this assignment; so why would you bet his job on your failure?"

"That's not what I meant, Chief," said Masters, as his brain became numb, again.

"Never mind," said Moore, as he walked towards the door. "Just don't fail." He then opened the door and slammed it shut. He then pushed the door open once more, and sharply said, "and leave this door open, some citizen or officer might actually need to talk to you."

When the Chief left, Masters, could hear the officers and visiting investigators in the squad room making muffled sounds of laughter, he could also see the smiles on their faces. He immediately slammed the door shut, then just as quickly re-opening it, as he remembered what the Chief had said. When he stepped into his office, the entire squad burst into laughter. Masters wisely decided not to humiliate himself any further, by reacting.

That evening Masters decided to leave a little early, in order to contact his bankers to find out what could be done about his missing money. He got into his personal vehicle and pulled out of the parking lot.

Jerod Spence notified James Banner, on a specially designed FBI communications system, that he was on the move.

"It's about time," said Banner. "My man has been waiting for his chance all day. He'll be in a new Corvette, red in color." He then gave Spence the tag number to pass on to his officers.

Masters had driven less than a mile to an established point, which was correctly pre-determined by Captain Spence as part of his route home. At that point Banner's informant pulled out at a high rate of speed from a merging street directly beside Masters, which caused him to swerve slightly to the right. Just as Masters' vehicle slightly crossed into the Corvette's lane, they slightly collided with Masters, hitting the Corvette's left bumper. The driver of the Corvette immediately smashed a large bottle of Jack Daniels Bourbon across his console which had been placed in the passenger seat for that very purpose. The liquor spilled all over the driver's clothing, as planned. The driver slammed on brakes and came to a sudden stop. He then opened his door, bumping Masters passenger door.

"What is wrong with you!" screamed the informant. "Are you drunk?"

"What's wrong with me?" Masters yelled back. "From the smell of things, it seems that you're the one who is drunk."

"You caused this," said the informant. "You're the one who hit my $45,000.00 car, causing this very expensive bottle of thirty-year-old Bourbon to break and spill all over me and my car. You are nothing but a stupid, and irresponsible driver." The informant then turned and yelled at a passing motorist and his passenger. "Hey, fellas! Could you get to a phone and call the real police, this guy is drunk; and I think he's impersonating a police officer."

The people in the vehicle, who were the reporter and his cameraman, tipped off by Banner, were driving slowly by the scene, as planned by Banner.

"Of course," said the cameraman. "Is anyone hurt?" They then pulled over to the side and pretended to contact their office to send for the "real police".

The driver, who was wearing a body-bug, and who had additional microphones secretly hidden in his vehicle, could be heard by members of the task force, members of Spence's Special Operations Unit, and the Chief and Major Schackelford.

"I love this guy," said Chief Moore. "Where did you find him, Jim?"

"I arrested him on a fake drug charge to get him away from some unsavory characters who were planning to kill him."

"Why were they planning to kill him?" asked Spence.

"Because they thought he was my informant, which he was." James Banner grinned. "I'll explain later."

Just as planned, Masters did exactly what was expected. He got on his radio and told communications to send one of his officers. One of Spence's officers was standing by.

"336 to radio!" Spence's officer said. "I'm close. Show me handling the signal 41, involving an officer."

Before Masters could say anything, radio responded "336 radio will show you handling the vehicle accident."

Unit 336, Officer Carl Watley, was one of Jerod Spence's top officers. He was also an expert in DUI cases and Accident Reconstruction. He was the perfect officer for this particular call. He knew exactly what to do and he knew exactly how to do it. He was also Spence's most loyal officer; and his brother-in-law.

"Unit 336," said Watley. "I'm 26 at the 41." Which simply meant that he had arrived at the scene of the accident.

"Received! 15;27 hours," was Radio's response; which meant that the unit's arrival time was 3:27 pm.

"336 to Radio," said Watley. "Is there a Lieutenant or higher close by, the officer involved in this 41 is Sgt. Hiram Masters.

As planned, Capt. Jerod Spence quickly responded and immediately went to the scene. The whole time that everything was taking place, the News camera was filming the incident. Masters continued to become more and more irate. He was anxious for someone to let the driver who hit him, know that it was the drunken Corvette driver's fault and the not his fault. He wanted the officer to just charge the guy with Driving Under the Influence; and then put him in jail. It was simple.

"It's an open and shut case!" Masters said to himself. "I wish this stupid officer would just get on with it." Masters' voice was a little louder than he intended it to be. Both the officer and informant overheard him and looked directly at him. Even the Cameraman, who was ten feet from the scene was able to pick up every word.

The driver of the Corvette, who was also the informant, looked directly at Hiram Masters and smiled. "It must really be hard on you, being the only 'smart guy' in a room?" Although he was smiling, his voice was cold and biting.

"It is when I'm around a bunch of imbeciles, like you," Masters said. He then looked at the officer, and turned red. "Oh, I didn't mean you, Officer."

"But you did mean to say that I was stupid," the officer said, very calmly.

"What do we have, Officer Watley?" asked Spence as he stepped out of his vehicle. He was careful to park his unit behind 336's patrol car, not to obstruct the News Camera's line of sight.

"At last! Someone who knows what to do," Hiram Masters blurted out.

Everyone, including the News Reporter, and Cameraman, just

shook their heads in total disbelief. "How can someone that dumb pass the Sergeant's exam?" the reporter asked the Cameraman.

"You're not going to believe it, but that imbecile was once a Captain," replied the Cameraman.

"You've got to be kidding," responded the reporter. "I know that APD has high standards. He must have had some strong political ties; or he slipped through the cracks big time."

"Just let Officer Watley do his job," said Captain Spence. "We'll figure this all out in just a few minutes. First of all is there anyone hurt?"

"Just my clothes," said the informant. "When he hit me, he broke my bottle of Jack Daniels across my console and got it all over me."

"Nothing personal," said Officer Watley, "but you do smell like your covered in alcohol. Do you mind taking a field sobriety test; and then blowing into this breathalyzer."

"Of course not," said the informant.

"I bet he blows at least a twenty," Masters scoffed. "We'll finally see just how drunk this guy really is."

"First of all," said Watley, "I need the driver's license and proof of insurance from both of you, to even begin this investigation!"

TWENTY-EIGHT

SERGEANT HIRAM MASTERS WAS SUDDENLY AWAKENED FROM A virtual mind-numbing drunken stupor by the pounding on the front door of his home. Matter was caked over his right eye; and his left eye would barely open. His head felt like it was slowly being crushed by a vice. He was still in his uniform from the evening before.

He literally fell out of bed and hit his left cheek on the end table, causing a deep cut to bleed profusely.

"I'm coming," He was able to yell out, as he rushed to the bathroom to grab a towel.

When he finally got to the door, he was a little surprised, but somewhat expecting, to see that Chief Bobby Moore, Major Johnny Schackelford, Major Jim Banner, and Major Jack Caldwell were all standing there.

In his never-ending arrogance, Masters blurted out, "Well, I guess this is my week in the barrel!"

"I guess you're right, because it is" said Moore, pushing his way past Masters and entering his living room. He then looked at Schackelford and calmly said, "Johnny, see if you can find some coffee in this unbelievably filthy place; and possibly put on a pot."

Major Schackelford nodded and pushed his way through the clutter in the living room and went towards the area, which appeared to be the kitchen.

"Where's your coffee and pot, Hiram?" Schackelford asked Masters.

"The pot is in the sink," Masters answered, with a harsh look of pain on his face. "The coffee should be on the top right shelf."

"Well, you did it this time, Sergeant!" said Caldwell, as he looked directly at Masters. He did everything he could to hold his composure and keep from jumping with joy. "I think you may have made the national news."

"What are you talking about?" Masters snapped.

"I suppose you haven't turned on your TV or radio." The Chief's voice was calm, but firm.

Masters shook his head. "I just woke up! What happened? What is this all about?"

Banner walked over to the large console against the center of the living room wall. He turned it on and flipped to the local news channel. The story of Masters encounter with his alleged drunk driver, was the top story of the day.

Masters wiped the crud from his right eye with his sleeve. He looked through blurred blood-shot vision at the reporter, who was giving a blow by blow description of the humiliating events of yesterday. Hiram Masters tried to study the scene, intently; but his eyes began to water, involuntarily. He immediately lit up a cigarette and moved closer to the TV.

"I don't understand!" He said, in total disbelief. "I can't believe this." He then squinted his eyes and moved even closer. "How could they have possibly gotten this footage?"

"If I were you," said Chief Moore. "I would not worry about how they got the footage. I'd be more worried about the fact that they have the footage; and it is an accurate description of what you did."

"I guess that means I'm finished?" Masters said to the Chief.

"That would be a correct guess," the Chief nodded.

After Masters was totally humiliated and completely emasculated. He simply hung his head; and put his hands over his face; and began to bawl like a baby.

"I can't believe this." Masters exclaimed. "WHAT HAVE I DONE?" He began to gasp through his intermittent jerks and sobs.

Johnny Schackelford shoved a large ceramic cup of black coffee in front of him. "Here, Hiram. Drink this. It might help."

Masters looked up at Schackelford, with pure contempt. "I don't need anything from you!" He snapped. "haven't you already done enough to hurt and humiliate me? I bet you and Banner are really enjoying this." His total hatred, disdain and scorn for the two of them, completely erupted. He then looked up at Schackelford in total disbelief as to what he had just uttered.

Major Schackelford calmly looked directly into Masters inflamed eyes and moved the ceramic cup closer to him. He then, with absolute composure, simply said, "Please drink this, Hiram; and don't say another word."

Masters acquiesced and slowly put the cup to his lips.

Although it had only been less than five minutes, it seemed like an eternity to Hiram Masters before Chief Bobby Moore spoke.

"We still need to move Herman Friday and his son to safety Monday morning," Moore said. "Spence tells me that you do have a full-proof plan in which to get that accomplished."

The chief then slightly turned in his chair to face Masters.

"I'm, officially, suspending you, without pay," said Moore, "at least as far as the news media is concerned and pending an official internal affairs investigation. I want you to turn over your badge and service weapon to Major Schackelford."

Masters grimaced as he did what the chief ordered.

"This may not exactly be the end for you, Masters," Moore said, seemingly sympathetic. "If Spence is right—and that is an absolute 'if'—he may have saved your career once again."

Masters eyes began to take on some life. "What do you mean, Sir?"

"If you can pull this off," said Moore, "you may have a shot at keeping your job."

Masters' face slightly lit up. He looked up at the chief, like a broken puppy. "I've always felt that Jerod Spence was the best officer I have ever known," Masters replied.

"Spence will be here in a couple of hours," said Moore; "to work with you. You will not go near the police station for any reason, whatsoever. Do you understand? You are technically suspended!"

"Yes, Sir!" said Masters. "You can count on it!"

"All of your business will be conducted from here. Captain Spence will take care of any support you might need."

Chief Bobby Moore then stood up and put on the most somber face that he could muster. "This is literally your last chance Hiram. If you mess this up, you're done. No one, not even Jerod Spence, will be able to salvage you. Do you understand?"

Masters stood up and awkwardly saluted. "I will not disappoint you, Chief!"

Moore only shook his head. He then turned and abruptly walked away. His entourage followed.

They waited until they were miles from Masters house before the entire group erupted into laughter.

"Johnny, you are one cold-blooded individual," said Caldwell. "The way you said 'and don't say another word' was pure elegance. It dripped with caustic sarcasm." Caldwell smiled. "It was vintage Johnny Schackelford!"

"That's the highest compliment you have ever paid me, Jack!" Schackelford responded. Thank you, my dear friend."

"I'm just glad," responded Caldwell, "that the rank hasn't gone to your head!"

TWENTY-NINE

AT 7:30 AM THAT MONDAY MORNING CAPTAIN JEROD SPENCE arrived at Masters' house. He then helped Masters to map out his "fool-proof" plan, which in fact Dr. Amy Griner had designed.

The plan had three basic components; which were two decoys and one actual transport. The first decoy would consist of two FBI agents, one agent who was the driver. A second agent who would pretend to be Herman Friday; and a young child, who would look like Clark Friday. The Clark Friday "look-alike" would slip through a hidden portal in the back seat into an area in the trunk, which was heavily armored and already occupied by a third FBI agent. The first decoy would then proceed on a pre-established route to a false safe house.

The second decoy would follow the same plan as the first, with the exception that the pre-established route would be much shorter than the first to another false safe house. Both the first and second decoy units would leave from two different houses. The third unit would follow the same design as the first two; but it was supposed to represent the actual transport. Unknown to Masters, however, all three units were decoys; but he was told by Capt. Spence that the third unit was the one which was carrying Herman Friday and his son.

"I thought that I was supposed to drive them to the safe house!" Masters arrogantly exclaimed.

"You were," responded Spence. "Until you appeared on national TV, showing your ignorance, to the whole country."

"How was I supposed to know that there was a film crew there?" Masters, defensively, answered.

"Whether they were there, or not," Spence shot back, "You should not have acted like a drunken sailor."

"You're right" said Masters, giving in almost too quickly.

It was at that moment that Spence realized why Sgt. Masters was very anxious not to waste any more time. He wanted, desperately, to be away from Spence; in order to call Kimbrel and let him know what was happening.

He wanted desperately to let him know that he would soon have the location of Friday and his son. When he had it, he would give Vernon the address only after Kimbrel brought him the million dollars he requested.

"Since you're so anxious to keep Herman and Clark safe, because your job is on the line," Jerod spence said to Masters. "I'll let you follow the third unit to the real safe house; but you have to keep your distance."

Hiram Masters smiled. Jerod Spence had just given him the perfect opportunity to locate the safe house and contact Kimbrel.

Masters then drove to a location, which was a short distance from the starting point of the third unit. He then sat in his car and waited for Spence to give the signal for the operation to begin. Exactly thirty-three minutes later Spence announced over his walkie-talkie that everything was a go!

At this point the plan had been perfectly executed. The only thing that remained, was for Masters to use his home telephone to contact Vernon Kimbrel. Once all three units had arrived at their respective safe houses; the mission seemed to be an absolute success to Hiram Masters. He knew exactly where Herman Friday and his son were. He could even see them get out of their car and go into the safe house.

"This is unit M one," said Spence, "to unit M two."

"Unit M two to Unit M one, go ahead," answered Masters, somewhat surprised.

"Unit M two," said Spence. "I need to make a 59 with you, as soon as possible."

Spence was asking for Masters' location, for them to meet. Masters immediately told Spence exactly where he was. He was sure that Spence was coming over to give him an "at a boy" for a job well done. Sergeant Hiram Masters was even more surprised by the next radio transmission, which he received.

"Unit One to Unit M two," said Chief Bobby Moore.

Masters could hardly contain himself as he grabbed the walkie talkie, and immediately; pressed the talk button.

Without thinking Masters blurted out, "This is one. Go ahead two. I mean this is two to the Chief." Out of pure frustration Masters completely abandoned all police radio protocol and simply said, "This is Sgt. Masters calling Chief Moore. Go ahead, sir."

The chief, who was doing everything he could to stifle his laughter, answered, "Unit M two call me from your home phone, after you meet with Captain Spence."

"I absolutely will," answered Masters.

After Masters arrived at his home, he immediately called Chief Moore.

"I just wanted to thank you for a job well done," said Moore. "I may still be able to save your job. I can't absolutely guarantee anything; but I feel relatively confident that the mayor will go along with me on this."

Masters thanked him, profusely, and without shame. "Thank you, chief. I will never let you down, again."

"You already have," the Chief said to himself.

As soon as they hung up, Masters called Kimbrel. "Okay, Vernon," Masters said. "I got the location."

"Well, where is it?" asked Kimbrel. "I also have Kirby Nox with me."

"What are you talking about? I said only you; and no one else!" Masters yelled into his phone.

"You also said," sneered Kimbrel, "That you wanted a million dollars. I don't exactly have that kind of money laying around; so, I had to bring Kirby in on it. Especially, since it is his money he wants to be there!"

"Okay!" answered Masters. "You made your point. I'll see you behind the Walmart, our usual location. I'll be there in about an hour. I have a couple of things I need to take care of first."

"Like what!" snapped Kimbrel

"None of your business!" Masters said, trying not to act his usual terrified self.

"I'll be there, with Nox, waiting for you," answered Kimbrel, with a softer, but very sarcastic voice.

They then hung up.

Capt. Jerod Spence knew exactly where the meeting would take place. He already had all task force members and the SWAT team members in place. Everything seemed to be working perfectly as Dr. Amy Griner had planned.

"That lady is a pure genius!" Spence said to himself.

Chief Bobby Moore looked at Major Johnny Schackelford and smiled.

"Well, Johnny," Moore said proudly, "It looks like our boys are going to do it this time!"

"I honestly think you're right!" said Schackelford. "This will be the culmination of one of the hardest, and most lengthy, investigations that this department has ever worked."

Moore nodded in approval; and he knew that they were nearing the end.

When Hiram Masters pulled up, James Banner and Jack Caldwell, who were watching the video feed from a SWAT surveillance van, could not believe their eyes. Masters was driving the same unmarked police unit that be had just used for the operation of transporting Herman and Clark Friday to their new safe house.

Little did Masters, Kimbrel, and Nox know that their prey was less than 400 yards from their location, secure in one of the most heavily armed and highly secured SWAT units in APD history. Banner and Caldwell had decided to bring Herman and Clark Friday with them to witness the takedown of Kimbrel and Nox. It was their hope that this would, once and for all, end their on-going fear and concern of the two thugs. Chief Bobby Moore and Major Johnny Schackelford completely agreed with them and ordered the highest level of security for them.

It was coming to an end and they did not want anything to go wrong.

THIRTY

As James Banner thought back to the beginning of the journey that he and Jack Caldwell had been through, over the past years, his mind went to his final year in college. Their first meeting with Vernon Kimbrel, through James Counter and Counter's wife, Sheila. A tear formed in his eye, as he thought about the brutal murder of both Counter and his wife, by Kimbrel.

"He's nothing but a psychopath!" Banner blurted out. "The world would be better off without him!"

"What?" asked Dr. Amy Griner. "Are you okay, James?"

Banner just nodded. "I'm alright," Banner responded, slightly embarrassed.

Dr Griner returned the nod, seeming to completely understand.

Major Banner also thought about his career with the Florida Times Union; and his friendship to City Editor, Brince Thomas; who would later become Executive Managing Editor. A friendship which would cause Banner's newspaper career to catapult to the highest levels of reporting. His career with the paper, however, would end abruptly, with the Kimbrel situation; and result in both he and Caldwell beginning new careers with the Atlanta Police Department. It was also his and Caldwell's deep friendship with Bobby Moore, now Chief of Police, and their loyalty to former Chief Herbert Jenkins, which brought them both to the high executive levels, which they presently held as Directors of the Metropolitan Atlanta Narcotics and Intelligence Task Force, which brought a smile to Banner's face.

"When this thing is over," Amy whispered to Banner, "you had better tell me about the thoughts you're having. They seem highly inappropriate; and I can't wait to hear them."

"I promise I will," Banner responded, with a smile. "I love you, Amy!"

"I love you, too, Jim!"

"Well, let's get the volume up on these monitors," interrupted Tony Watson. "I also want to see how well this 'state-of-the-art' recording device works."

"It's working perfectly," said the SWAT tech. "The sound is clear and crisp; with absolutely no distortions." He then looked directly at Watson. "Sir, I must say that you Feds get the very best equipment."

Watson smiled. "Son, after we blew the first John Gotti trial because of faulty, low quality recording equipment, both the Director and the Attorney General decided to set aside the low bid concept, when it came to intelligence equipment. They only wanted the very best of the highest quality. So, here we are."

"Spend more on the equipment," said the tech, "so you won't have to spend millions on a trial and lose it."

"Exactly!" said Watson. "Son, you would make an excellent FBI technician."

Both Banner and Caldwell looked directly at Watson. "You will not talk to that APD tech anymore. We are not going to let you steal one of our top IT officers away from us."

"Just kidding!" said Watson, raising both hands in surrender.

Dr. Amy Griner moved close to Tony Watson, her fiancé, and kissed him gently on the cheek. She then smiled and softly said, "Tony remember that you're in a heavily fortified SWAT van. Surrounded by heavily armed SWAT officers; who are more than likely, the top officers in the entire state, if not the country. So, if I were you, I'd re-examine my idea about 'kidding' about recruiting one of their officers, if you want to leave here with all of your limbs intact!"

The entire van broke out into muffled laughter, and abruptly stopped when they were interrupted by Masters' voice and face on the monitor.

"Well, do you have the money I asked for?" Masters asked.

"Here's your 'blood money'," said Nox, getting out of the passenger seat of the car, carrying a very large metal brief case. "Exactly one million dollars, as you requested."

"Okay," said Masters. "I'm going to count it and hide it; and I'll be back in an hour or so to give you the address."

"No, you're not!" said Kirby Nox, "as he stuck a Browning 9mm, semi-automatic in Masters' face and stuck it against his forehead. "I'm sick and tired of this 'cloak and dagger shit. You're going to check the money, right now. Then you're going to give us the address; and we'll leave here happy; and you'll leave here rich. Do you understand?"

"There's something wrong!" said Jerod Spence, speaking through the special communications walkie talkie unit to the other members of the SWAT and Task Force Units on sight. "Sniper one, do you have a clear shot on Nox. I don't like the way he sounds."

"Affirmative," answered sniper one. "A perfect shot to the back of his head. No chance of collateral damage."

"I guess that means he probably won't kill Masters," said Chief Moore, "when he kills Kirby Nox."

"That's exactly right," said Johnny Schackelford. "Don't look so downhearted. Hiram Masters is going to wish he was dead, when this thing is over."

"I know you're right," laughed Bobby Moore. "It's just that this could be wrapped up in such a nice neat package; if something like that were to happen." A smile crossed the Chief's face. "I know that it would absolutely be wrong, and a sin, to hope for something like that; but it sure would be efficient; and expedite everything."

"And the explaining would be little to none," said Schackelford.

Chief Bobby Moore vigorously nodded, in agreement. "You're going to make an excellent Assistant Chief of Police; and a great Chief, as well, Johnny. You have my philosophy; but you're your own man. Have I told you how proud I am of you?"

"Many times." Answered, Major Schackelford, and I'm lacking in the words to tell you how much I appreciate it; and how dear you are to me."

"Now don't get 'weepy eyed' on me," said Moore, as he stood and embraced his dear friend, Johnny Schackelford.

Suddenly they were interrupted by Jack Caldwell's voice over the monitor, which the FBI had put in the Chief's office, as a courtesy.

"Jerod, remember," said Caldwell, "he has to hand either Kimbrel or Nox the address for us to have Masters on a conspiracy to commit murder charge."

"I understand, Sir," said Spence. "That also means we can then charge him with the attempted murder of that US Marshal."

"Correct!" answered Caldwell.

"Everyone continued to hold your positions at the ready," said Spence. "Sniper One! You can relax and get a cup of coffee."

Suddenly all of the SWAT team members, and the Task Force members, especially Caldwell and Banner, as well as, Chief Moore and Major Shackelford, went into near catatonic shock.

"What is he doing?" Moore blurted out.

Schackelford just shook his head in total disbelief.

"Just kidding," said Spence. "I thought I'd like to try a little humor for a change. Sniper One, disregard my last order. Continue to mark Nox."

"Roger, Sir!" Sniper One answered.

"I didn't think that Captain Jerod Spence had a sense of humor," Shackelford said.

"We'll be taking down one of the most violent murder syndicate in the South," said the Chief. "I guess we should allow him at least one joke."

They both laughed.

"But you're right," said Moore. "I honestly did not think he had any kind of a sense of humor."

THIRTY-ONE

SERGEANT HIRAM MASTERS THEN LOOKED UP AT KIRBY NOX AND pretended that he had finished counting the million dollars. "Well, looks like it's all here," he said. "So, since you kept you're end of the deal, here's the address." He then took off his shoe and pulled a folded piece of paper from the bottom. He then handed it to Nox.

Kirby Nox opened the paper, read it; and handed it to Kimbrel. "Do you know where it is; and does it look right to you?"

Vernon Kimbrel read the note; and a big smile came across his face. "I know exactly where it is," he said. "Since all of his other information, in the past several years has been exactly correct; I know that we can trust him on this."

Masters smiled with the vote of confidence, which Kimbrel had bestowed upon him.

"That cold blooded traitor." said Caldwell. "Did you get that, Chief?"

"Every disgusting word, Jack!" said Moore, with contempt in his voice. "that worthless slug, with a badge, has been giving a serial killer information for several years." Moore shook his head in total disbelief. "The DA's going to have a field day with this; and the APD is going to take a beating; but we are doing the right thing."

"Maybe we can dump some of the blame on the FBI," said Banner, with a big smile on his face.

Watson turned and looked directly at Banner, until he saw the smile. "We'll be glad to do it for you," said Watson, smiling back at Banner.

However, even the most perfectly laid out plans can have the most unpredictable variables, that cannot be expected. What happened next was one of those situations. It was not something that anyone really wanted; but it did turn out to be the best scenario.

"Sniper one! You have a green light!" called Captain Jerod Spence. "He just cocked the hammer to his Browning!"

"I got him," Sniper One responded, as he pulled his trigger. The back of Kirby Knox's head exploded; but unfortunately, so did the barrel of his Browning 9mm. The bullet entered directly into Hiram Masters forehead, knocking him backwards; and splattering his brains across the passenger window, and door panel. killing him instantly.

Capt. Jerod Spence raced to the scene and slammed on brakes just inches from the two vehicles. At that very moment Vernon Kimbrel, who looked shaken and panicked, jumped from the driver's seat and pointed his weapon at the SWAT commander. He then fired. The bullet struck the outside of Spence's vehicle door, which was now open and protecting Spence.

Spence immediately leveled his shot gun and fired. He was obviously a much better shot than Kimbrel. His double-ought, buck shots first smashed the driver's window sending the shards of glass, and shots deep into Kimbrel's upper chest and groin area. The vicious serial killer fell backwards, screaming.

"I'm hurt, damn it." Kimbrel's voice was sporadic and labored. "It's bad. I'm dying. Help!"

The entire scenario went down in a way that was totally unexpected. The most unexpected element, however, happened next, with Herman Friday. It was also the most unpredictable of all. The Swat Van pulled up to the scene just thirty seconds after Spence. When it stopped, Herman Friday rushed to the back door of the van. The SWAT officers were rushing out of the van in an effort to aid Captain Jerod Spence. Herman Friday was rushing with them.

Banner immediately grabbed Friday by the arm.

"What do you think you'/re doing," James Banner screamed in total disbelief.

Friday looked up at him, then glanced towards Clark.

"He's dying, Jim!" Herman Friday's voice was strained and conflicted. "Don't you understand? He's going to die without the saving grace of his Lord and Savior. We've got to do something to try and stop that."

"Have you lost your mind?" yelled Caldwell. "That guy is the worst serial killer, ever. He even tried to torture and kill your own child. You can't be serious. You can't possibly want to save his soul, Herman?"

"I absolutely don't," Herman said in a very determined voice. "Right now, I have absolutely no desire to save that man's soul. In fact, it's the one thing that I abhor the most. The thought of doing that makes me want to throw up; but I have to."

He then pulled loose from Banner's grasp and ran to the side of Kimbrel's dying body. Vernon Kimbrel appeared to be struggling to speak. He continuously gurgled and spit blood with each attempted word, as he gasped for life.

"Vernon, listen to me, please," Friday's voice was filled with love and compassion; as he knelt, next to Kimbrel's fatally wounded body. "You're dying; and you're about to go to face God's eternal judgement. I think you know that; but you don't have to be condemned. You can be saved! Just put your trust in our Lord, Jesus Christ. Accept Him as your living Savior and ask His forgiveness."

Kimbrel looked directly at Friday, with eyes of pure evil. He then moved his head faintly to the left, motioning Friday to move closer, which Herman did. Kimbrel slightly lifted his head, and began to speak his last words on earth.

"You can," Kimbrel's words were caustic and barely audible; but his next words were miraculously clear. "tell your God that He can talk to me at judgement time; and you can kiss my…", blood suddenly gushed from his mouth and ears, and his head fell backwards

His pupils suddenly turned darker, almost black, and seemed to cover his entire eyeballs. He then took on a look of absolute horror. His body twisted to the left, and emitted blood curdling screams from his mouth.

Herman Friday quickly jumped back, as he watched Vernon Kimbrel start to shake and contort violently. The screams continued, and became more like those of an animal. Suddenly they stopped, as his face took on a look of hopelessness. His eyes then became empty; and Herman Friday watched, as Vernon Kimbrel's tortured soul slipped from his body and entered into his chosen eternity.

"I don't understand," said Captain Jerod Spence. "why did you feel like you had to try and save him?" Spence was truly asking the question. "He would have never tried to help you or anyone else."

Herman Friday looked up at him and simply answered. "I know, Captain, but it's what God wanted me to do."

Every single person there humbly bowed their heads; and then immediately rushed to Herman Friday. They either embrace him or touched him. Most held back the tears in their eyes; but some didn't, as they openly let their tears flow down their cheeks.

Clark rushed to his daddy and held on to him for dear life. They both sobbed and cried relentlessly, and without shame.

"It's finally over," thought Herman Friday, as he embraced his precious son. "It's finally finished!"

James Banner walked over to Herman Friday and embraced him. "I promised you that I would take care of Clark, and I will do that, if that is still okay with you?"

"Of course," said Friday. "I will always love you, Major Banner, for all that you have done to save both me and my son. I promise to spend the time I have left on earth praying for you and your family. I'll also continue to ask God to forgive me for all the harm that I've done."

Banner immediately put his arm around Friday. "Listen to me, Herman. You only have to ask God to forgive you once, and then repent. God does the rest. You're forgiven; and God forgets your sins. He blots them out. They are as far away as the east is from the west."

He then smiled at Friday. "Do you understand?"

Thirty-Two

Chief Bobby Moore looked, at Major Johnny Schackelford, and his voice was very subdued; "I suppose we've had the very best scenario we could possibly have," he said. "I honestly believe that, morally, God really wanted Herman Friday to save Kimbrel."

"I agree, to a point," said Schackelford. "If we keep in mind that we, as human beings, can do nothing to save another human being. We can only bring them to Jesus Christ, by giving them the information of salvation. Then we've done our job. Herman Friday did his job, and he did it very well."

Chief Moore nodded in acknowledgement and agreement.

"It was then up to Kimbrel," continued Schackelford, "to either accept or reject what Our Lord was offering him, through the words of Herman Friday. If he accepted it, then God was ready to bring him into heaven; the blood of God's only Son, Jesus Christ, would have covered all of Vernon Kimbrel's sins."

"That would have been a lot of blood," the Chief said.

"I agree," Shackelford responded, slightly smiling.

"Well," said Bobby Moore, "we have to do something for those heroes out there, including Herman Friday. Since your position of Assistant Chief of Police will be effective tomorrow; that will become one of your new responsibilities."

Johnny Shackleford's jaw almost dropped to his knees, eyes wide as saucers.

"What?" Schackelford responded in shock. "Tomorrow. This is the first I've heard about this."

"I knew there was something I forgot," said the Chief, smiling from ear to ear. "You know how I am, Johnny. I totally depend upon you to keep me straight on things. I wanted this to be a surprise; so, I couldn't exactly tell you."

Assistant Chief of Police Johnny Schackelford immediately embraced Chief of Police Robert Moore; and the Chief returned his embrace.

"I don't know what to say," said Schackelford.

"How about 'thank you'?"

"Thank you, Chief."

"It was my honor."

The next four days primarily involved questions and answers, which were brought on by the news media. It also was filled with many calls of congratulations to Assistant Chief of Police Johnny Schackelford, by various members of the department, who were either sincere, or wanted some special favor from him. Chief Moore helped him to separate the two.

The Assistant Chief, also, made all of the arrangements for everyone involved in the Dixie Mafia dismantling, to receive a special MEDAL OF VALOR. These were presented at a banquet, which was given by the Mayor of Atlanta.

Hiram Masters was also given a medal of meritorious service, posthumously. This was done, with the approval of the Mayor, to prevent any further inquiries into Masters' position in the investigation. It was also done to keep his family from any further embarrassment.

As Chief Moore had said earlier, "It was the best possible ending for the Police Department!" Chief Moore and Assistant Chief Schackelford had to explain and re-explain their position, on numerous occasions, to the rank and file, who knew the truth about Masters, until everyone finally understood and agreed to accept the situation.

"Does this mean that the Metropolitan Atlanta Narcotics and Intelligence Task Force is breaking up?" asked Dr. Amy Griner.

"Not by a long shot," said Deputy Chief of Police, James Banner. "Both Deputy Chief Caldwell and I have been given so much additional responsibilities, that it takes two Deputy Chiefs to handle them."

"Either that," quipped Amy, "or the department realizes that it takes the two of you to come to a reasonable decision."

The entire office bursts into laughter.

"You know she's right," Caldwell responded.

James Banner nodded, in agreement.

James Banner went on to become the Chief of Police and Jack Caldwell, as expected, became his Assistant Chief of Police. Dr. Amy Griner was now Dr. Amy Watson. She and Tony officially adopted Clark Friday.

Clark had entered the Southwestern Theological Seminary, studying to become a Minister of God. He stated that he wanted to do it in honor of his mentor, James Banner.

Herman Friday became a prison chaplain. All his death sentences were commuted by the President of the United States. Unfortunately, he was murdered, by a former member of the Dixie Mafia, while he was in the penitentiary.

Fortunately, however, this former mass murder and serial killer lead over 400 prisoners and their families to accept Our Lord Jesus Christ as their Lord and Savior before his death.

I suppose that each life has its own intrinsic value. Both Herman Friday and Vernon Kimbrel saw themselves as being valuable, in accordance to their own perception. Friday, however, came to the final realization that there was one force far greater than any other desire he could ever have; and that was love. The overwhelming love for his son Clark; which finally led him to the path of salvation.

Kimbrel's love, however, was very twisted, as was his sense of justice. His egotistical, self-centered, love of his own desires cast him into the pit of hopelessness, where, in all probability, he now spends eternity.

THE END